I said I would drive. That meant, of course, that Lior would be riding on the back.

He was cool with that. And I was cool with him being cool. Let's face it, how many guys would be secure enough in their masculinity to be seen riding a bike behind a woman, their backs up against the sissy bar?

Lior turned out to be a great passenger. With an extra two hundred pounds on the back, the driver has to subtly shift his or her riding maneuvers. Most passengers, unfortunately, are literal backseat drivers. They try to anticipate your moves, try to shift their own weight when you lean into a curve. Then you have to shift in the opposite direction to keep from going down.

But Lior didn't do that. He just let me have complete control, going with my moves instead of directing them. I started to wonder…if he was that way on a bike, would he be that way in bed? Not an unappealing prospect.

Miriam Auerbach

Miriam Auerbach was born in Prague, Czechoslovakia. The first of many changes in her life occurred at age six, when she witnessed tanks rolling past her family's home during the Soviet occupation of 1968. Shortly thereafter, her family fled to the United States. She grew up in Denver, where she studied diligently to become a particle physicist. However, during a brief stint at Los Alamos National Lab, she began to suspect that building nuclear weapons just might not be the best way to spend her life. Thus, at age twenty she rebelled and spent the next decade living on the fringes of the Harley biker world.

In her thirties she returned to semiconventional life, earning a Ph.D. in social work and becoming a university professor. In this capacity, under the name of Miriam Potocky, she has taught legions of students and written a slew of academic treatises crusading for social justice for the world's dispossessed. She has found this to be a rewarding career, but one fine day she crashed headfirst into the glass ceiling of the ivory tower. Falling into a funk, she took to her bed to eat chocolates and watch old *Dirty Harry* movies. She didn't get Harry's appeal until she suddenly had a vision of him as a woman, and thus Dirty Harriet was born.

Miriam lives in Boca Raton, Florida, with her killer corgi, Elvira. She continues to profess by day and decompress by night by writing her next Dirty Harriet mystery.

DIRTY HARRIET
RIDES AGAIN

MIRIAM AUERBACH

DIRTY HARRIET RIDES AGAIN

copyright © 2007 by Miriam Potocky

isbn-13:978-0-373-88140-6

isbn-10:   0-373-88140-1

TheNextNovel.com

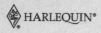 HARLEQUIN®

PRINTED IN U.S.A.

From the Author

Dear Reader,

I have three goals for this book:

1. To make you laugh
2. To make you think
3. To make you channel your own Dirty Harriet to be the strong, resilient, empowered woman you are

If I've accomplished any of these, let me know at miriam@miriamauerbach.com.

In sisterhood,

Miriam Auerbach

To Karen Dodge
Who sees the invisible,
Hears the ineffable,
Touches the intangible.

Acknowledgments

Thanks to my agent, Paige Wheeler;
my editor, Tara Gavin; and everyone at Harlequin.

CHAPTER 1

As weddings go, it was a little…unorthodox. And that was before the body turned up. But I'm getting ahead of myself.

Let me begin by stating immediately and emphatically that it wasn't *my* wedding. Please, that's not gonna happen (again). At thirty-nine, I've been happily widowed for four years since shooting my abusive husband in self-defense. That act of freedom really made my day and earned me the nickname Dirty Harriet.

My real name is Harriet Horowitz. The wedding in reference was that of my best buds, Chuck and Enrique. Now, seeing as these are two members of the male persuasion, some people would say it wasn't a real wedding. To them I would say, "Get a life!" Love doesn't get any more real than what these two had going.

Okay, so our beautiful, bountiful burg of Boca Raton and our great state of Florida doesn't bestow legal recognition on gay unions. As far as I'm concerned, that's a plus. After all, it was the law that had sanctified my own unholy sham of a marriage. And it was the law that had done shit for me when my husband beat the shit out of me.

So the law, rules and regulations don't mean a whole lot to me. Truth and justice do. That's where my inner vigilante comes in. But more on that later.

Chuck and Enrique's love was true and just, which is why I was there that April Sunday standing up for them as best human in their commitment ceremony. I was standing, to be precise, at the altar of the Church of the Gender-Free God, waiting for the grooms to walk down the aisle.

In honor of the occasion, I had ditched my daily uniform of black leggings, black tank top, riding boots and leathers when I dismounted my trusty steed—my 2003 hundredth anniversary Harley

Hugger. I wore a rented Vera Wang floor-length silver gown, matched by four-inch sandals and shoulder-length silver earrings. I'd had my normally wild dark hair blown out, and it hung down my back in long silky perfection. My green eyes were fully lined and mascaraed, and my normally bare, raw nails were painted Princess Pearl. Damned if I didn't look like my former incarnation of myself— a Boca Babe ne plus ultra.

What's a Boca Babe, you ask? Well, that's a two-part question. First of all, the town of Boca is located between Fort Lauderdale and West Palm Beach and has been called the Beverly Hills of the East. Just like that other place, Boca's got its balmy breezes, plentiful palm trees, mind-boggling mansions, serious shopping and beaucoup bucks. So much money that Boca ranks as the second wealthiest municipality in Palm Beach County, just behind the island of Palm Beach, which is in a whole different class. Think Monte Carlo and St. Tropez. Or, Palm Beach is old money elite and Boca Raton, tacky nouveau riche. And most of Boca-ites' new money seems to come from some pretty shady dealings.

Now as for Boca Babes, here are some clues: If it costs you $200 to get your hair cut and another $250 to get it colored, you might be a Boca Babe. If you don't talk to anyone who doesn't own anything made by Prada, then you just might be a Boca Babe. If your boobs are a size 34DD and your butt is a size zero, then you are probably a Boca Babe. If you live in a house the size of a jumbo jet hangar, then you are likely a Boca Babe. But if you don't have a husband who's a doctor, lawyer, investment banker or developer raking in over a million a year, then you're definitely *not* a Boca Babe. And if you're all of the above but have hit the big 4-0, you're no longer a Boca Babe—you're now a BOTOX Babe.

I shed my Boca Babe persona like a snake shedding its skin the day I shed (okay, shot) my husband, and I've never looked back. Now I'm a hog-riding, ass-kicking, swamp-dwelling private eye making a fine living busting the very people I used to wine and dine with. So my temporary reversion to Babeness gives you some sense of the supreme sacrifice I was making for my friends.

But even though I'd transformed myself for the day, a part of the real me still came through, like the rose tattoo on my left boob that peeked out of my low-cut dress, thanks to the strapless push-up corset that I'd spent a small fortune on. Between that and a pair of my old Gucci high heels, I was in some serious discomfort. After all, I wasn't 21 anymore. This whole hottie act does not get easier with time. I was ready for this show to get on the road so I could disrobe.

The proceeding seemed to be taking its sweet time, though. So as I waited, I gazed out at the guests. Right up front was Enrique's mama from Panama, decked out in a lime-green chiffon gown with a matching broad-rimmed hat. She was absolutely beaming at the prospect of her baby boy finally settling down. As Chuck's family had long since disowned him due to his perceived sin against God and Nature, his surrogates were there. There was my mother, Stella Celeste Kucharski Horowitz Fleischer Steinblum Fishbein Rosenberg, who had recently unofficially adopted Chuck as her honorary son, which made him, I guess, my honorary brother. Mom was all gussied up, as usual, in a butter-yellow cocktail dress with her hair perfectly coiffed in a helmet around her face. She'd beamed with approval when she'd arrived at the church and seen my reclaimed Boca Babe look. I guess she figured my titty-baring getup would finally snag me a man to replace her late, unlamented son-in-law. Of course, she had failed to consider that I had no interest in a replacement, and even if I had, many of the guys at this gathering were batting for the other team.

Next to Mom sat her new squeeze, Leonard Goldblatt, in a white summer suit with a gray tie to complement his gray brush cut. They had met on a cruise a couple months previously. Leonard was a former CIA agent, and as such I'd initially had my suspicions about his intentions toward Mom. But then I'd actually met him and my guarded apprehension turned to grudging appreciation. Yeah, okay, maybe I'd been guilty of premature evaluation. But wouldn't you feel the same if your own mother's vulnerable feelings, and fortune, were at stake? As it had turned out, Leonard was good for my mother. But forget about that; the man was good for me. His relationship with his own grown children was of the supportive and noninterfering variety, and some of that had rubbed off on Mom.

On Leonard's other side was Boca's big-time benefactress, the Contessa von Phul, who sat regally, dressed in her usual Chanel suit and pearls, her sleek mahogany pageboy completing the picture of a perfect seventy-year-old BOTOX Babe. I'd recently solved a murder case for her, during which she'd met Chuck and Enrique and wangled an invite to the big event. Never far from her side, the contessa's Chihuahua, Coco, sat primly in her lap, all duded up in a pink rhinestone collar.

Next to the contessa was Guadalupe Lourdes

Fatima Domingo. Lupe, as she was known, was a cultural anthropologist who also had had a role in the contessa's case, and in the process had become a good friend of mine. Today she wore a traditional Mexican embroidered dress and her salt-and-pepper hair was elaborately swept up with multicolored ribbons. The outfit was an homage to her hometown heroine, the late artist Frida Kahlo.

Beyond the front row sat an assortment of Chuck and Enrique's friends and acquaintances, including their gay matchmaker, who savvily saw this event as a supreme marketing opportunity and brought along all his clients. There were also all the straight bad boy bikers from Chuck's maintenance shop, the Greasy Rider, and from the local biker bar, Hog Heaven; and all Enrique's coworkers from the Boca Beach Hilton, where he was the hotel dick, that is to say, the chief of security.

Outside, I heard the unmistakable rumble of Harleys. Ahhh…the day's musical entertainment had arrived, in the form of the Holy Rollers Motorcycle Club and Gospel Choir, a group of five black drag queens whom I had met at the rehearsal dinner the previous evening.

I knew they rode their hogs in full riding gear, so it would take them a while to change into their wigs, makeup, bras, girdles, gowns and all. So I would be standing here in my misery a while longer. I tried to take a deep breath to send some healing oxygen to my aching back and feet, but my chest wouldn't expand beyond the rigid steel cage of the corset. I coughed and staggered, drawing all eyes to me. Great. Like I really wanted to be the center of attention here. Apparently, my cough provided some kind of permission to the assembly to engage in similar behavior, as there followed a flurry of throat clearing, foot shuffling, seat adjusting and other expressions of discomfiture.

Finally, the nuptial procession started with the entrance of the first of the Holy Rollers, Cherise Jubilee. She came down the aisle in a red sequined clingy sheath and a headdress piled high with fake cherries, à la Carmen Miranda.

She was followed by Virginia Hamm, wearing—

you guessed it—a pink gown crisscrossed with brown threads and studded with what looked suspiciously like cloves. May the Gender-Free God help us. Next came Keisha LaReigne, wearing an egg yolk-yellow caftan streaked with reddish-brown strips and a bejeweled golden tiara nested in her bouffant hair. Close on her heels was Lady Fingers, in a vanilla-colored off-the-shoulder number that split into separate panels from her waist down to her knees.

The four Holy Rollers lined up next to me at the altar, awaiting the arrival of their final member, Honey du Mellon, before they would launch into their harmony. But she was nowhere to be seen. Nervous titters passed through the assembly as we waited. Finally, she rushed in, out of breath. She'd managed, miraculously, to prop up a set of knockers the size of…well, honeydew melons. If her supporting infrastructure was anything like mine, I could see why she was out of breath. But apparently that wasn't the reason. Arriving at the altar, she puffed, "So sorry, loves. My hog had some mechanical trouble on the way over. I just got here and changed as fast as I could. Okay, ladies, let's rock and roll!"

With that and a nod to the organist, they launched into "We Shall Overcome." Now, this particular selection, as I understood it, was an homage to the Church of the Gender-Free God and its founder, the Reverend LaVerne Botay. The good reverend had grown up attending the Dexter Avenue Baptist Church in Montgomery, Alabama, in the fifties, listening to Martin Luther King, Jr. preach the social gospel of service to the world's oppressed. Like the late great martyr, she'd rejected religious fundamentalism in favor of the Golden Rule.

Now, personally, I wasn't a particular believer, being the progeny of my dearly departed Jewish daddy and my very present Catholic mom. The only thing I'd gained from that interfaith union was a double dose of guilt. However, I respected the hell out of the Reverend Botay's message and mission. As the Holy Rollers sang out their souls, tears came to my eyes.

But they weren't because of the words. They

were because of the organ. The damn thing was way out of tune. In fact, it was downright blood-curdling.

The Rollers were rolling their eyes at each other. I decided to roll with the punches. After all, every wedding has something go wrong. It would all be a fond memory in our collective future.

As the Rollers launched into another spiritual, Chuck and Enrique came gliding down the aisle, hand in hand. Dark-eyed, dark-haired, clean-shaven Enrique was his usual slick and dapper self in his Armani tux. No surprise there. But Chuck… Well, any description would only be a gross injustice, and as I said, this whole celebration was about justice. So suffice it to say he was in an identical tux, all 250 redneck pounds of him. His graying goatee lent him a distinguished air, and his bald pate gleamed with what I chose to believe was pure delight, not nervous perspiration.

As the happy couple reached the altar, the Rollers, with perfect timing, ended in glorious harmony: "Free at last, free at last. Thank God Almighty, we are free at last."

Yes! Thank God Almighty I would be free at last of this sartorial straitjacket, not to mention the grinding organ noise. Just as soon as the Reverend Botay arrived, the vows would be exchanged, the blessing bestowed, and we'd all be outta there and off to the reception at Hog Heaven.

So, okay…where was she? Minutes passed as we all looked nervously at each other. Okay, I know I said all weddings have snags, but enough was enough. I'm an investigator, after all. With a "don't worry, I'll take care of this" nod to a baffled-looking Chuck and Enrique, I set off to investigate.

I headed past the altar where a door led to the back rooms. The door to the reverend's office was halfway open. Just as I was about to rap on the door, I saw her. The poor woman was crumpled behind her desk, her violet-and-white vestments flowing about her petite body. Rushing over, I could see clear as day her skull had been smashed in and her black hair was matted with blood. The murder weapon was lying right next to her, also covered with blood. A big metal organ pipe. No wonder that monstrosity was emanating those bloodcurdling screeches.

Bile came up my throat. I ran into the adjoining bathroom and dry heaved in the toilet. I couldn't believe it. The last two weddings I'd attended had both ended in murder. Maybe marriage really was a dangerous proposition. Yeah, okay, so I'd been the perp last time, blowing away my husband at a friend's wedding reception. But how could this be happening to me again?

Then my conscience, always a little slow on the uptake, came on line. What the hell was I doing feeling sorry for myself? A good woman, a woman of peace, had been savagely slain.

It was time for Dirty Harriet to take charge. I pulled out my cell and called the cops.

CHAPTER 2

I couldn't leave the scene until the police arrived, so I had no choice but to call Enrique on his cell and brief him on the situation. God, how I hated to do this to him and Chuck on their big day. Enrique handled it with perfect calm, composure and decisiveness, just as I knew he would, security pro that he is, which is why I'd chosen to call him instead of Chuck. Although Chuck looks awful mean and imposing and outweighs Enrique by a good hundred pounds, in reality he's a teddy bear and it's Enrique who's the rock in the relationship.

Enrique said he'd handle everything in the church sanctuary while I stayed at the crime scene. Frankly, I thought I got the better end of the deal. I could just imagine the hysteria that would ensue among the guests when they heard the news. I'd rather be alone with a dead body than with a bunch of drama queens—male or female.

Naturally, while waiting for the police to arrive and begin their official investigation, I began my unofficial one. I looked around the room. The office walls were covered with plaques and certificates honoring the reverend's many charitable deeds for the community. There were no signs of struggle. Apparently, the reverend had been attacked unawares. Her desk bore the usual materials one might expect: desk pad, pen holder, telephone. There was a bible with an accompanying concordance and prayer book. A red velvet binder contained the homily for today's wedding ceremony. A pair of reading glasses, undisturbed, rested beside it.

I returned to the bathroom that adjoined the office, but nothing was amiss. Then I stepped outside the office door, which opened onto a corridor. I took a few steps out, staying close to the office door so that no one could enter without my seeing them. The room to the left of the office was a kitchen and on the right was a small meeting room containing about ten chairs arranged in a circle. This was where the Holy Rollers and I had changed from our biker gear into our ceremonial wear. I had draped my own street clothes over the back of one of the chairs, and I saw that the Holy Rollers had done the same. Except only four of their outfits were there. One was missing. What was that about?

Taking a final quick look around the room from the doorway, I saw something I hadn't when I'd been there earlier. A panel on the back wall had been slid open, revealing the huge pipes of the organ. So the instrument backed up to this room. I could see where one of the pipes had been yanked out. That must have taken a lot of strength. Maybe the kind fueled by rage. Then, apparently, the killer had gone to the reverend's office and bashed her head in, probably while her back was turned.

At that moment several uniformed and plain-clothes police officers arrived at the reverend's office door with a heavy clomp of footsteps. I went over to meet them. One of the plainclothes, a stocky, ruddy-faced man, seemed to be in charge.

"I'm Detective Reilly," he introduced himself. "You're the one who called this in?"

"Yes. Detective Harriet Horowitz."

"Excuse me?"

I handed him one of my business cards that identified me as the sole proprietor and operator of ScamBusters Investigations. They Scam 'em, I Slam 'em, read the inscribed motto.

Reilly glanced at the card, then back up at me.

"Right," he said, somewhat sarcastically, I thought. "Now you wouldn't be harboring any ideas about interfering with an official police investigation, would you?"

"Of course not. You see right there, I'm a scam specialist, not a murder maven." Hey, that was a perfectly true statement. Yes, I'd solved a homicide case for the contessa, but one murder does not a maven make.

"Right," he said again. "Okay, Ms. Horowitz, I'm

going to ask you to step into another room so I can interview you while my officers secure the scene and collect evidence."

"Fine," I replied and stepped back.

"I take it the scene has been undisturbed since you discovered it?"

"Of course."

"Good. Webster!" he called out. "Set up the crime-scene tape. Martinez, start taking pictures. Duchamp, get the forensics going and call the medical examiner. Now, Ms. Horowitz, I understand there's a large gathering of people in the chapel?"

"Yes, that's right."

"Hernandez, Tomaso, start the interviews in there," Reilly barked. Then to me he said, "I see there's a kitchen over there. I could use some coffee. Why don't we go sit in there?"

"Fine," I said again. I was being uncharacteristically agreeable. But then, there was nothing for me to be disagreeable about. That is, until we entered the kitchen and Reilly looked at the empty coffeepot, then looked meaningfully at me. Did this dude seriously expect me to sashay over and make coffee for him? Yeah, right. I looked meaningfully right back at him. He walked over to do the job himself. Hey, at least we understood each other.

When the coffee was done, he asked, "Would you care for some?"

"Sure," I said. "Black. No frilly stuff."

He poured each of us a cup and we sat down. Now this was more like it. Being served by a man was my idea of gender equality.

"So, tell me what happened," he began.

I told him, omitting, of course, my own snooping activities. When we were done, he said, "Okay, Ms. Horowitz, thank you for your statement. You may join the others in the chapel. If we have any questions for you later, we'll be in touch."

He rose and then he even took the coffee cups to the sink and rinsed them out. I was impressed. Maybe under his leadership, the cops could solve this case all by themselves without the aid of my own spectacular investigative acumen…. Nah.

I returned to the sanctuary, where the guests

were all now seated apart from each other in separate pews. Two officers were interviewing Keisha LaReigne and Cherise Jubilee in separate corners of the large chapel. Apparently, they'd ordered all the guests not to leave and not to speak to each other while they grilled each one.

Chuck and Enrique slumped a few feet apart in a pew, looking utterly defeated. My mother, drama queen extraordinaire, was sobbing hysterically. Leonard looked at her helplessly, unable to console her, since talking was prohibited. The contessa sat quietly but ramrod straight, stroking Coco's ears. She—the contessa, not Coco—was one cool cucumber. Lupe was fingering a rosary and chanting to herself. I knew she was a *bruja*, or Mexican witch, so I figured she was attempting to infuse positive energy into the macabre affair.

We all sat there for two hours until the officers had talked to every single one of us. Then Reilly came in and announced, "Ladies and gentlemen, you are all free to go. Except for Mr. Harrison."

Who?

Then we watched in amazement as Reilly walked over to Honey du Mellon, slapped a pair of handcuffs on her and said, "Trey Harrison, you are under arrest for the murder of the Reverend LaVerne Botay. You have the right to remain silent...."

The rest of the Holy Rollers started screaming.

"Lord have mercy!"

"Sweet Jesus, save this poor soul!"

My mother wailed, "Leonard, Harriet, do something!"

Chuck collapsed into Enrique's arms and sobbed, shaking convulsively.

The contessa and Lupe clasped hands and stared at the floor in silence. Coco leaped off the contessa's lap and ran between the pews, yelping and whining. The church sanctuary boasted several large glass sculptures by the renowned artist Chihuly, and the little bitch ran right into one of them. It teetered precariously on its edge before one of the biker guests made a sudden dive, saving the Chihuly from being chipped by the Chihuahua. The contessa yelled for Coco to come to her side.

The commitment pageant had turned into complete pandemonium.

"Ladies and gentlemen, calm yourselves!" Reilly ordered. "We will not tolerate public disorder. Those who are unable to peacefully leave the premises will be taken into custody."

As I said, this guy was good. Silence descended like a mourning shroud.

"Now, since you will all find this out soon enough from the media," Reilly said, "I'll advise you now that we have sufficient probable cause to arrest Mr. Harrison. We found his street clothes in a Dumpster just outside the church. They were covered in blood. Our preliminary crime-scene tests have determined that the blood is the same type as the victim's. Mr. Harrison has admitted that he was wearing a pair of Tommy Hilfiger chinos, a Ralph Lauren polo shirt, and a leather motorcycle jacket and boots this morning."

A cop spewing off fashion-designer labels. Only in Boca.

"Yes!" Honey screamed. "But I'm innocent! I

changed from my street clothes in the little meeting room just like everyone else. I left my clothes there with everyone else's and came in here!"

"Shut up, Honey," Virginia Hamm snapped.

"But I didn't do it! Can't you see I've been framed?"

"Zip it!" yelled Lady Fingers.

But Honey wasn't listening. "What about fingerprints? You know mine aren't on the murder weapon!"

"Not that we are obliged to share any details of the investigation," said Reilly, "but there are no prints on the weapon. It was wiped clean. So that does not exonerate you. Furthermore, there were no witnesses to your claimed actions."

"Of course not, you nimwit! I told you I arrived late because of bike trouble, so no one saw me change."

By this time the contessa had corralled Coco and now she came up to Honey and stood regally before her, clutching the cowering canine.

"Ms. du Mellon—I mean, Mr. Harrison—you will now cease to speak. Mr. S. Lee Dailey will be paying you a visit in the county facility shortly. All your future communications will come solely through him."

Yowza! The contessa's poise and power never ceased to amaze me. S. Lee Dailey was Palm Beach County's most notorious criminal defense attorney. He had gotten off one lowlife who'd grabbed a little old lady's handbag and dragged her to her death with his car as she'd hung on to the bag for dear life. Another of his clients was acquitted in the murder-for-hire of his socialite wife. In other words, S. Lee Dailey was a total sleazeball completely devoid of morals and ethics. Exactly what you wanted in a defense lawyer.

Evidently, while everyone else had been in hysterics, the contessa had gotten Dailey on the horn and gotten him to agree to see Honey. Apparently, Honey was as impressed with the contessa's actions as I was because she did finally shut her trap. The police hauled her off.

Now I had a dilemma. Among all the distressed wedding-party members and guests, whom should

I calm down first? Chuck and Enrique? My mother?
The Holy Rollers?

The hell with prioritizing, I thought, and made
an executive decision.

"Everybody, please be seated," I stated loudly.

There must have been something in my tone
because miraculously they all obeyed. I climbed up
the altar to the lectern and faced the congregation.
Then this alien, authoritarian, ministerial personality took charge.

"Let's have a moment of silence for the
deceased," I said. Again they obeyed, after which I
resumed my oration.

"Dearly beloved, we were gathered here today to
celebrate the love of our cherished friends. Now an
atrocity has shattered our joy and plunged us into
sorrow. But in our shock and grief, we must not
compound this horrific act by relinquishing that
quality that has brought us together today—our
compassion for each other. Although Chuck and
Enrique's ceremony has been disrupted, their love
will endure. And all of us, too, must endure."

I was picking up wind, and sailed right on.

"While I did not know the Reverend Botay very well, I knew her well enough to feel confident in saying that she would want all of us to go forth and live her message of the trifecta, um, I mean triumvirate: hope, charity and faith. Faith that her killer, whoever it may be, will be brought to justice. So please, go in peace and honor the reverend's memory through reflection on her good works and through comforting ministration to each other in this time of despair."

With that I stepped down from the lectern.

"Amen, sister!" Cherise Jubilee cried out.

"Hallelujah!" Keisha LaReigne chimed in.

The congregation lined up to give their condolences to Chuck and Enrique.

After the guests filed out, I went over.

"I'm so sorry, guys," I said.

"Hell of a speech, Harriet," Chuck said. "But now what are we gonna do?"

"We'll reschedule the ceremony," Enrique said matter-of-factly. "Nothing can tear us apart."

"What about our honeymoon?" Chuck said, as fresh tears pooled in his red, swollen eyes. "We were supposed to leave tomorrow for a week in San Francisco and the tickets are nonrefundable."

"You know what?" I asked. "I think you guys should go on your honeymoon. It will do you good to get out of town. Go and comfort each other. When you get back, you can start making new wedding plans."

"I think you're right," Enrique said. "Come on, Chuck, let's go tell Mama, then we'll take her home and pack. She's catching her plane back to Panama City tomorrow, too."

Chuck rose silently, his head hanging. Enrique and I stood and I hugged them both goodbye and wished them a healing journey. Apparently, I was still possessed by the minister's spirit. Then I hugged Enrique's mother, the contessa, Lupe and each of the Rollers.

Finally I went over to Mom and Leonard.

"Harriet, that was such a touching oration," Mom said, dabbing a Kleenex to her eyes. "Why, I could hardly believe that was my daughter speaking. I'm very proud of you."

Great. I undergo a total personality transformation and now my mother is proud of me. Thanks, Mom.

Leonard's eyes met mine, and he gently touched Mom's elbow.

"Let's go home, Stella," he said.

"Yes, all right, honey. Harriet, come with us. You shouldn't be alone at a time like this."

"No, I'm okay, really," I said. "You two go on."

I gave her a reassuring hug and they departed.

I collapsed on the altar steps. Damn, I didn't know what had possessed me. But now that I was dispossessed, I was drained.

Finally, I took my own advice and collected myself to depart. I went back to the small meeting room to change so I could ride home. The whole corridor was cordoned off with yellow crime-scene tape and two cops were standing guard.

"I just want to get my clothes," I told them.

"Sorry, ma'am," one replied. "We can't release them. They're crime-scene evidence."

Great. I'd have to ride my low-rider in this low-cut outfit. I didn't like the idea of riding practically nude, but at that point I just wanted to get home.

I stepped outside the church. Immediately, I was assaulted with a burst of camera flashes. What the hell? Blinded, I grabbed at the handrail on the church steps. When my eyesight returned, I saw that a throng of media vultures and curiosity seekers had gathered. Ignoring all the yelled requests for comments, I walked toward my hog in the parking lot. On the way, I saw a big white van labeled Crime Scene Investigation.

"Hey!" somebody yelled. "Are you with the TV show?"

That stopped me.

"Huh?" I asked.

"*CSI: Miami.* Didn't you know that's what they're filming here? We're looking for David Caruso. Have you seen him?"

"Huh?" I repeated. "What are you talking about? Caruso's been dead for almost a century."

"Not the opera singer, silly!" some old bag with a

ton of makeup on her wrinkled face giggled. "David Caruso, that hot actor? Get with the times, chickie!"

Okay, so I wasn't up on the latest shows and celebrities. That happens when you don't own a TV. But this was unbelievable. "This is not a TV set, you morons!" I snapped. "This is a real crime scene!"

"Really?" somebody whined. "Bummer. We were so hoping to see him."

With that the crowd dispersed, grumbling in disappointment.

I couldn't take any more. I pulled my dress up to my crotch, mounted my hog, and put on the helmet that I'd stored in my saddlebag. I turned on the ignition, shifted into gear, and roared off toward my tranquil swamp abode. I just had to get the hell out of Boca, that weird twilight zone where reality and fantasy collide, where truth really is stranger than fiction.

CHAPTER 3

As I rode my hog, grooving with its V-twin vibe, I began to chill out. Wellness on wheels. The bike does it every time. By the time I reached the end of solid ground where the Everglades murky swamp sprawled before me, I was high on the hog. The greatest high there is.

My customized airboat was docked, waiting for me. I pulled down the boat ramp, pushed my bike up onto the boat and tied it down. Then I pulled the ramp back up, put in my earplugs, covered them with my soundproof earmuffs, and started the deafeningly loud engine. The rear-mounted fan started spinning and I took off across the River of Grass.

The Glades are a wetland equivalent of the Sahara: vast, foreboding, constantly changing. The river shifts like the desert sand dunes. The water level rises and falls as it's released from Lake Okeechobee, creating new tree islands and submerging old ones. For those unfamiliar with this environment, it's easy to get lost and disappear. And the swamp is unforgiving. A decade ago a DC-9 jet exploded over the Glades. The pieces fell into the swamp and were sucked right into the mud underneath. Barely a trace was found.

It's only the rare that dare to live here. Like the nomads of the desert, Glades dwellers are a breed apart, finding sustenance in a place others deem uninhabitable.

To me, that sustenance is for my soul. I'd escaped here after the nightmare of my marriage and its deadly demise. I'd left everything behind: my humongous house, my clothes-filled closets, my Mercedes and all the pampering perks of the Boca Babe life. I'd had to do it to recover from the Boca Babe addiction—and my ex-husband's abuse.

Now home is a two-room wood cabin on stilts. The little place is totally self-sufficient, with its own generator, water supply and septic tank. All I really need to survive. My only connection to the outside world is my cell phone.

When I got to the cabin, I tied up the boat, went inside and pulled off my boots. Now, as any addict knows, recovery is an ongoing process. Sometimes you get cravings for your old comforts. This was one of those times. As I poured myself my nightly shot of Hennessy in my crystal glass and sat down on the porch, self-pity started to set in again.

I'd had one hell of a day. And I had no one to comfort me. Chuck and Enrique had each other; Mom had Leonard; the Holy Rollers had each other; the contessa had Coco; and Lupe had her witches' coven or whatever the hell it was. Poor me.

A splash of swamp water startled me out of my self-pity. Suddenly I felt better. Oh, yeah, I did have somebody. My next-door neighbor, Lana. There she lurked, all six feet of her, her black alligator eyeballs staring straight at me.

The cold-blooded beast had a warm spot for me. She always read my thoughts and knew just the right thing to say. This time it was "Hey, ditch the pity party. After all, you chose this loner lifestyle, didn't you? So deal with it." Now, I didn't say she always said the sympathetic thing, just the right thing.

"Yeah," I said. "Damn right. I did choose this and I wouldn't trade it for all the bounties of Boca. Besides, I was more alone among all that luxury than I am now."

At that, she flipped her tail and took off. I finished my high-class cognac and turned in.

I WAS STARTLED FROM A DEEP slumber by a ringing sound that kept going and going. My eyes flew open. My heart was pounding and my sheets were soaked with cold sweat. Where was I? What time was it? What was that noise?

Then consciousness flooded back and I remembered. I'd been having a nightmare. A replay of the day I shot my husband at a friend's wedding reception. I guess yesterday's events had triggered it this time.

The nightmare is always the same. I'm sitting at a table in a ballroom filled with five hundred guests.

My husband, Bruce, yells at me, then raises his fist, something he's never done in public before. Suddenly, after ten years of abuse, I realize it will never change. Unless I change it. I reach into the pocket of Bruce's jacket, which is on the back of a chair that he's knocked to the floor. I grab the gun that I know is there, the one he's been carrying for a while now, in his cocaine-induced paranoia. I aim the gun at him and say, "Go ahead, make my day." And when he lunges at me, I blow him away.

I shook myself and came back to the present. I was safe now in my remote cabin. I looked at the clock. It was six in the morning. And that noise? Oh, it was my phone.

"Yeah," I grumbled into the receiver.

"Harriet, Laurence Williams here."

"Who?"

"Cherise Jubilee."

"Oh, right. Sorry."

"No problem. Listen, the ladies and I would like you to meet with us at my office at nine this morning. We have an urgent proposal to discuss with you."

I rubbed my eyes.

"Yeah, okay. I can do that. Where's your office?"

"The Smile Wide Dental Center." He gave an address on Federal Highway in Boca.

"What? You want me to go to a dental office? They're torture chambers. I go for my cleanings every six months, and that's it. Avoid them like the plague."

"Actually, it's the plaque you want to avoid," he said. "Nonetheless, Harriet, as I am a dentist, I am indeed located in a dental office. If it's such a problem for you, I can give you a mild tranquilizer when you arrive. It's standard procedure for my patients with dental anxiety."

Jeez, just how much of a wimp did he think I was?

"As long as you stay away from my teeth that won't be necessary. See you at nine."

I had my coffee, showered, dressed and piloted the airboat to land. I pushed my hog off the ramp, suited up for the ride with the extra pair of leathers I kept at home, and took off. The hog, like my swamp dwelling, is part of my reincarnation from beat-up Boca Babe to unbeatable Brainy Broad. Dominating a five-hundred-pound dynamo gives you one hell of a head rush. Actually, a total body rush.

I arrived at the dental office and was escorted to a back room, doing my best to ignore all the treatment rooms along the way, with their drills and pliers and other tools of torture.

I was shown into a lavishly appointed conference room. The four Rollers were seated around a long, oval polished wood table. Today they were in their alternate guises as professional men and upstanding members of the community. They reintroduced themselves with their real names: Richard Johnson (Virginia Hamm), a short bald man who, I recalled from our initial meeting at the rehearsal dinner, was an accountant; Herbert Graham (Keisha LaReigne), a portly wine importer; James Carmichael (Lady Fingers), a thin prep-school teacher; and, of course, Laurence, the dentist, and a tall one at that. And at the head of the table sat none other than S. Lee Dailey, an imposing figure with a barrel chest, beefy hands and a bulldog face.

"We appreciate your coming, Harriet," Laurence began. "As we're all busy, I'll get right to the point. We are completely outraged over the wrongful arrest of Trey. We know he was framed, and we want to hire you to find the real killer. Right now Trey is still in custody pending a bond hearing. Mr. Dailey here has agreed to represent Trey and he is in full agreement with contracting your investigative services to assist the defense."

Dailey issued a grunt and a nod.

"But gentlemen, uh, ladies, whatever, murder is not really my thing," I protested. "There are plenty of other P.I.s in town that can handle this."

"None that will care like you, that will sink their teeth into it and not let go till the job is done," Laurence said.

Had he just compared me to a rabid dog? I wasn't sure whether to be flattered or offended. But he continued.

"You come highly recommended by the contessa, and that's more than good enough for us."

"Well, thanks. But what makes you think Trey was framed?"

"Think about it, Harriet," Richard said. "Anytime there's a crime committed and there are any black men within a five-mile radius, the police have no problem quickly apprehending a suspect, right?"

"Well, yeah, you may have a point...."

"Plus the fact that we are a bunch of queers does not incline the police to view us impartially," Herbert added.

"Yeah, okay, I can see how you're in double jeopardy, being black and gay, not the most favored groups in our great society. But what about Trey's bloody clothes that were found in the Dumpster?"

"If you recall," James said, "Trey is a prominent local criminal judge. Not that you could tell by the way he was running off at the mouth yesterday, but the poor dear was beside himself. But notwithstanding that brief lapse of judgment, would he really be so stupid as to commit a murder and leave the evidence so near the scene?"

"Um, I suppose not. And the church was open during the ceremony, so anybody could have come in, put on Trey's clothes, killed the reverend, and then dumped the clothes."

"Exactly," Dailey finally spoke up.

"Furthermore," Laurence said, "the police have come up with the most ridiculous motive. All of us are out of the closet, except Trey. He's always feared that his sexual orientation would jeopardize his judicial appointment. Mind you, he's not on the down low, he's just not out."

"Pardon?" I asked. "The down low?"

What the hell was that? That stupid style where guys wore their pants waists down around their knees?

"Girlfriend, don't you watch the Bravo channel? Or *Oprah*?" Herbert asked.

"Uh, no." I didn't bother informing them that I don't own a TV.

"'The down low' refers to black men who are outwardly straight. They have wives or girlfriends, but keep secret gay lovers on the side," James, the teacher, lectured.

"Right," Herbert said. "So Trey is on the up-

and-up, not on the D.L. He's not stepping out on some poor unsuspecting sister. He has a long-term male partner, he's just not public about it."

"Okay, so what's this got to do with a motive?"

"Get this," said Laurence. "You know the Boca City Council is voting on a proposed same-sex marriage ordinance in the next few weeks."

"Yeah, I've read about it." I'd also seen the protesters in the streets. The public battle had been getting increasingly nasty.

"LaVerne was a very public proponent for the ordinance," Richard said. "She was a major target of the opposition. She'd received death threats."

"Now here's what the police are saying," Laurence continued. "They claim that LaVerne threatened to out Trey in order to promote her own pro-gay agenda, the idea being that if the public found out that such a prominent and respected member of the community was gay, they'd be more inclined to support the ordinance. So, the police say, Trey killed her to prevent his outing.

"Now that is such a load of horse pucky," he

went on. "LaVerne would never have outed anyone. That would be totally incompatible with her beliefs. So we think the antigay protesters murdered her and framed Trey. If Trey gets the death penalty, then they'll have killed two birds, an uppity black woman and a gay black judge, with one stone, er, organ pipe. Could there be a more perfect setup?"

Without waiting for a reply, he went on. "So, will you take the case?"

"Let me think about it," I said.

I thought for about half a second, then said, "Yes, I will."

After all, despite my numerous protests about not being a homicide heavyweight, I'd already embarked on my unofficial investigation. This case was personal. I'd liked and admired the reverend and everything she stood for. I had found her body. My best friends' ceremony had been ruined. And, above all, the Rollers had now raised my ire over the world's gross injustices.

My inner vigilante was tapped and set for takeoff.

CHAPTER 4

"Great!" Laurence said. "Here's where we think you should start."

Now, I generally don't take well to being told what I should do, but I let that pass for now.

"The Boca City Council is holding a public hearing on the same-sex marriage ordinance tomorrow," Laurence went on. "We think you should attend and check out the key players."

"Sounds reasonable," I said. Then I couldn't help myself and went on, "But I think I'll look into some other angles in the meantime. And I'll bring a contract for you to sign tomorrow morning."

"Okay," he agreed. "Thank you all for coming. Now let's all get back to our jobs."

We shook hands all around, which seemed more

fitting in this setting, as opposed to the theatrical hugs we'd all exchanged yesterday. Then we departed.

Outside, I put on my helmet and rode my hog to my office. It's located just outside the Boca city limits, along a seamy stretch of Highway 441. It's a one-room deal with grated windows in a strip mall right between Tony's Tattoos and Carl's Checks R Us. Far from Boca glam, but just right for my upscale clients desperate for discretion about being scammed.

I went inside and sat down at my desk. I propped my feet up and proceeded to think. I felt that I needed to keep my mind open to all possibilities, and not pursue the antigay angle single-mindedly. The Rollers might well be right about that, but I couldn't let that bias me at this early stage of the investigation.

Any murder investigation needs to begin by looking into the life of the victim. So I decided to start by interviewing the Reverend Botay's parishioners to find out more about her.

I called Lupe, who I knew was on the church's board of directors. She and I had been developing a friendship over the past couple months. Although this was threatening to my loner sensibilities, another part of me was drawn to our connection. So instead of launching right into business, as is my usual MO, I did the friendship thing by asking how she was doing.

"I'm very distraught," she said. "I've got this huge hole in my heart where LaVerne used to be. I miss her so much." She burst into tears.

Oh, boy. Now I had to play the role of comforter? Scary. I wasn't sure I had that skill. As a Boca Babe, *friendship* had meant one-upmanship. Or rather, up-womanship. It was all about who had the best clothes, the best house and the best (read: richest) husband.

But I wasn't a Boca Babe anymore. I realized that part of my recovery meant forging real relationships instead of faux friendships. So I plunged in.

"How about getting together for lunch?" I ventured. "It might help you to talk about your grief."

Wow, I surprised myself with that one.

"Oh, that would be really nice," she replied. "Thanks so much, Harriet. You're a true friend."

Who, me? Was I really worthy of the honor? I took a deep breath. Yes, I could do it. Dirty Harriet was up to any challenge.

We agreed to meet at one at a restaurant on the Intracoastal. Actually, the place referred to itself not as a restaurant, but a *dining concept*. Give me a break. But it was the location I was going for. Gazing at Florida's gorgeous blue-green waterways always had a calming effect on me, and I figured it might for Lupe, too.

I spent the next couple hours wrapping up a scam investigation for a health insurance company. The claims processors had suspected that several local doctors were doing medical up-coding, meaning giving patients diagnostic codes that were for worse conditions than they actually had, thereby squeezing higher reimbursements out of the patients' health insurance. The bust had been pretty simple. I'd gone into all the doctors' offices with a tape recorder in my purse, complaining of flu symptoms. The diagnoses of my condition variously came back to the insurance company as pneumonia, asthma, pulmonary fibrosis and so on. Now, those old boys were facing criminal indictments.

When I finished my final report and invoice for that case, I rode back to the east (read: desirable) side of town to meet Lupe.

She was already waiting for me at the restaurant. I could see she really was in bad shape. Her face was drawn and pale. She didn't have on her usual Frida Kahlo-style makeup, hairstyle and jewelry, and she wore jeans and a T-shirt instead of her traditional Mexican attire.

"You've got to eat," I commanded.

Now where the hell did that come from? I had no maternal instincts or nurturing behaviors. Or did I?

We took a table right by the water and ordered some Bahamian conch chowder and a couple grouper sandwiches.

"I'm so sorry for your loss," I began. "I didn't really know the reverend personally, but I sure liked what I did know about her. Do you want to tell me about her?"

"Sure," Lupe said. "She had a huge heart. Her

whole congregation was her family. And she loved to feed people. She really followed Jesus's teachings. You know how he said something about 'when you feed the least among you, you feed me'?"

No, I didn't know, but I nodded, not wanting to interrupt her.

"She just loved to have people over to her house for soul food. And it really was exactly that. Feeding the body with ham hocks, greens, black-eyed peas and okra, but feeding the soul at the same time with her love. Or maybe, Jesus's love coming through her."

"Uh-huh," I said, trying not to sound skeptical. This religious stuff really wasn't my bag. But now that I was in this investigation, I'd have to tolerate it.

"She just radiated peace and joy," Lupe went on. "And, you know, she didn't have an easy life. Imagine growing up black in the segregated South, just when the civil rights movement was happening, with all its lynchings, school bombings and so on. Then becoming a woman preacher, then becoming outspoken and breaking away to form her own nonconformist church. You can imagine all that didn't sit well with a lot of people. I would think she must have felt very alone at times, but I guess not. I guess she had the faith that God was always with her. Her inner peace in the face of such trials was an inspiration to so many, me included."

"But I thought you were a witch," I said. "How come you were also a member of her church?"

"Witchcraft doesn't exclude any other religions. It's about nature and harmony, not about doctrine. And, of course, LaVerne was inclusive of everyone, as well."

A tear slid down Lupe's cheek.

"I loved her. I miss her. I'll never forget her."

"Neither will I," I said. "I will find her killer. I won't let her death, and her life, slip away into oblivion."

"What do you mean?" Lupe asked. "Are you investigating the case?"

I explained about the Holy Rollers hiring me.

"Oh, I'm so glad," Lupe said. "What can I do to help?"

Her eyes lit up and I could see that she immediately felt better at the prospect of taking action.

"You already have, by telling me about her," I replied. "So tell me more. You said the congregation was her family. But was there anyone else—husband, partner, children?"

"No, she really didn't seem to have a personal life. Her work was her whole life."

"Did she talk about any problems, concerns, or fears in the days before her murder?"

"Not to me. As a matter of fact, she was ecstatic about a major donation that the church received recently. She announced it to the congregation last Sunday, the one before yesterday. Dennis Pearlman donated $250,000 to the battered women's counseling program that the church runs."

I knew the name. Pearlman was one of Boca's obscenely wealthy residents, the owner of a vitamin manufacturing company. He was well known for his charitable, and highly publicized, contributions to the community, so this didn't seem like anything unusual.

"Okay. Anything else you can think of?"

"No. I wish I could."

"Can you give me the names of some other members of the congregation who might know something?"

"Absolutely," she said. She pulled out her Black-Berry, looked up some names and phone numbers, jotted them down and handed them to me.

"Oh, I almost forgot," she said. "We, the board, that is, have made arrangements to have La-Verne's funeral on Wednesday. We don't have the time yet, but I'll let you know as soon as we do. It'll be at Mort's. And we'll be having a potluck gathering at my house afterward, so please come."

I knew Mort's well. Mort was my late stepfather and his Mort's Mortuary and Crematorium was the biggest operation in town.

"Of course, I'll come. But I'm surprised the police are releasing her body so soon," I said.

"I guess they've done everything they need to do," she replied.

"Okay, I'll go call the congregation members now," I said.

"Thanks, Harriet. I really do feel better already."

"I'm glad," I said.

I paid the lunch bill, refusing her insistence on splitting it. Then we shared a hug and departed.

I went back to the office and called the people on the list. Unfortunately, none of them could provide any further information beyond what Lupe already had.

By then it was getting late and it seemed as if there was no more I could accomplish that day. So I headed home to mull things over with Lana the Gator.

As always, she was an attentive listener as I sat there on my porch with my Hennessy and recounted the day's events.

"So what'd you think, that you'd find the killer in one day?" she snapped.

"Well, of course not. Okay, maybe," I admitted.

"Persevere," she ordered as she floated off into the sunset.

"Thanks for the support," I muttered.

Then, since I'd been in such a friendly, supportive state all day, I dialed Mom to see how she was doing.

"Oh, Harriet, it's so thoughtful of you to call," she said. "Of course, I am still completely traumatized. But Leonard is here with me, being a complete doll. He's the best thing that's ever happened to me."

Well, I'd heard that one a few times before, what with Mom's multimarried past, but I kept my mouth shut. And mentally patted myself on the back for it.

"You've heard that the reverend's funeral is at Mort's on Wednesday?" I asked.

"Yes. Of course, we'll be there."

Then she pulled out the big one.

"Now let's talk about something less depressing. Why don't you come over for dinner with Leonard and me one of these days soon? And bring your friend."

That last word was drawn out and emphasized.

There it was. Mom was once again trying to ignite my romantic life.

I knew perfectly well whom she was referring to, but feigned ignorance.

"What friend?" I asked.

"Lior, of course. Who else? Don't play games, honey."

Me, playing games? Please. Just exactly what was she doing?

Lior Ben Yehuda was my tall, dark, hard-body instructor of Krav Maga, the Israeli martial art of street fighting. Lior was an Israeli ex-commando whom I'd met while I was still a Boca Babe and married to Bruce. My personal trainer had suggested I take up Krav Maga for fitness, so I'd enrolled in Lior's studio. And as it turned out, it was Krav Maga that gave me the guts to gun down Bruce and end ten years of abuse. Not that Lior had encouraged that. But his training had transformed me from a victim to a victor.

So Lior knew about my past—how I'd married Bruce, an aspiring attorney, right out of college and was sucked into the Boca Babe addiction. Then Lior had witnessed my recovery from Babeness—

leaving the megahouse, the Mercedes and the clothes to the creditors, selling my jewelry to buy my hog, moving to the swamp, getting an office job for a private eye, and finally getting my own license and opening ScamBusters.

So I'd known Lior for a few years now. He wasn't intimidated by my Dirty Harriet persona; in fact, it seemed to turn him on. However, I'd kept up a good shield of denial of the simmering attraction between us. For one thing, following my murderous marriage, the last thing I wanted was another romantic involvement. For another, Lior was thirty years old to my almost forty. Even though I still had my looks, if not the artificial enhancements, from my Boca Babe days, I felt awkward about the age gap. But recently I'd experienced chinks in my longstanding armor. Lior and I had gotten together a couple times lately outside the fitness studio, and I'd made the mistake of telling Mom about it.

So something was happening between Lior and me, but I sure as hell wasn't ready to dive into something serious. And, of course, dinner at Mom's with him would mean exactly that.

"No, Mom," I said. "That's not happening. I'll come to dinner, but not with Lior."

"Oh, Harriet," she whined. "You've got to move on, honey. Lior sounds like a lovely young man and it's time you let down your guard a little."

I was about to come back with a nasty retort when I heard Leonard in the background.

"Stella, sweetie, why don't you let up a little? Harriet is a grown woman. She's fully capable of making her own choices. Let's just enjoy a dinner with her. We'll have a nice time."

Yeesss! Man, did I like this man.

"Very well, Harriet," Mom said stiffly. "I'll get back to you with a date. In the meantime, we'll see you at the funeral on Wednesday. Goodbye."

As I hung up, my mind wandered back to those two outings—I refuse to call them dates—with Lior. The first one had been at the local gun club, where we'd teamed up in a mixed-doubles target-shooting competition—Lior with his Israeli-made

Uzi pistol and me with my all-American Smith &
Wesson .44 Magnum, the one that used to be
Bruce's and that I now carry concealed in my boot.

We'd won first place. After that he'd asked me
to go out to celebrate our victory. I'd told him our
trophies were celebration enough but he'd kept
needling me every time I went to the studio to
work out until I'd finally agreed.

Then another battle of wills had ensued—where
to go, how to get there, what to do? The thing is,
Lior and I didn't seem to have a whole lot in
common except street fighting, sharpshooting and
sensual simmering. His taste in music ran to seven-
ties disco, while I was into Madonna and Shania.
That is, when I listened to music, which was rare,
since I usually preferred the sounds of the Everglades bog or the Evolution Hog. Lior liked to
watch the sunrise after staying out all night; I liked
to watch the sunset before sleeping in all night. He
was an observant Jew; I was an observant gumshoe.

We'd finally agreed we both didn't mind eating
and didn't mind the ocean. So we'd decided on a

brunch at the Breakers, a fancy-ass hotel in Palm Beach, the exclusive island where old money from the Northeast and Midwest comes to while away the winter months.

I'd said I would drive. That meant, of course, that Lior would be riding on the back. He was cool with that. And I was cool with him being cool. Let's face it, how many guys would be secure enough in their masculinity to be seen riding a bike behind a woman, their backs up against the sissy bar?

So one Sunday morning we took the ride up the coast. Lior turned out to be a great passenger. With an extra two hundred pounds on the back, the driver has to subtly shift his or her riding maneuvers. Most passengers, unfortunately, are literal backseat drivers. They try to anticipate your moves, try to shift their own weight when you lean into a curve. Then you have to make an unnatural, compensatory shift in the opposite direction to keep from going down.

But Lior didn't do that. He just let me have complete control, going with my moves instead of directing them. I started to wonder…if he was that way on a bike, would he be that way in bed? Not an unappealing prospect.

He also didn't wrap his arms around my waist the way you see so many women do when riding behind a guy. If passengers can't keep their hands to themselves without falling off, they have no business riding.

So we were in sync as we took in the dazzling ocean views. Eventually, we arrived in the thriving necropolis of Palm Beach. I swear, all those ocean-front homes up there look like mausoleums. It's the Land of the Living Dead.

When we got to the Breakers, I pulled right up to the opulent entrance. There was a time when the Breakers would have run bikers off the property, but now that the rich have co-opted Harleys as a status symbol, the hotel is more than happy to display hogs right up front alongside the Rollses and Bentleys.

We proceeded to the outdoor terrace overlooking the beach. We ordered a couple Bloody Marys and took it all in: the ocean waves, the white sand, the swaying palms, the blue sky. Damn, another day in paradise.

We didn't talk a lot. I figured I'd done plenty by even agreeing to go out. Actual conversation would take it to another level. One where I wasn't sure I wanted to be. So, we just enjoyed observing the social milieu. The Breakers was plenty entertaining. That day, it seemed as if half the population of New York City had come down for brunch, judging by the accents of the crowd. And apparently, when those New Yorkers were told they were going to a family reunion at the Breakers on the Island, most of them thought they'd heard *Rikers Island*. Evidently, they'd been looking forward to seeing the godchildren and such in the prison cafeteria, when, to their utter bewilderment, they found themselves in this strange place that bore a bizarre resemblance to the Doge's Palace in Venice.

As Lior and I sat there on the terrace, we eavesdropped on the conversation at the next table. This guy was saying, "Jeez, Ma, why'd you have Uncle

Luigi fix that mess I got into back in eighty-seven? Lookit how I could be livin' large here at Rikers, instead of busting my balls—" At that point, his sister smacked him upside the head.

"No, you numskull!" she cried. This is *the Breakers*, not *Rikers*! Now look what you did, Ma's upset!"

"Huh? Mazola spread? Yeah, sure, pass it over. You know how health conscious I am," the guy said as he forked a deep-fried cheeseball into his mouth and chased it with a shot of Southern Comfort.

Then there was the house band. In keeping with the Palm Beach locale, they were…well, how can I put this? Undead. They looked as if they'd been rooted in that same spot since 1954 and hadn't changed their tune since. I think they called themselves Vincent Zamboni and the Zombies.

So, all in all, Lior and I had a good time. There was only one minor snafu, when the server brought Lior ham instead of the steak he'd ordered. Since Lior kept kosher, ham was out. But he'd been totally charming and gracious in asking the server to take the meal back and bring another. And I had to admit that scored points with me. What a contrast to my ex (okay, dead) husband, who would have thrown a fit and made a complete ass of himself under similar circumstances.

My Breakers reverie was suddenly interrupted by Lana making an inauspicious reappearance.

"Hey, girl," she said. "I know you're hot to trot with Lior. But think about it. He knows all about you, but what do you really know about him? You admitted you didn't talk much. Did he actually tell you anything about himself?"

"Well, no, I guess not."

"So for all you know he could be a killer or something."

That gave me pause.

"Well, I'm one," I replied. "He doesn't hold that against me, so if he's one, which he isn't, why should I hold it against him? I'd rather hold him against me."

"Yeah, right," Lana said. "Just don't let your hormones run off with your judgment." With that she flipped her tail and took off again, this time into the darkness.

CHAPTER 5

The next morning I dropped by Laurence's dental office to have him sign the contract for my services on behalf of all the Holy Rollers. He informed me that Trey had been released from jail on a million-dollar bond put up by the contessa. I decided to talk with him later.

Afterward, I proceeded to the city-council meeting to check out the antigay protesters. I arrived at City Hall and went into the council chamber. It was an auditorium with rows of seats for the audience and a dais up front supporting a large curved table for the council members. I was a little early and only a few others had arrived. I sat down in the back row so that I would be able to observe everyone.

A couple minutes later, someone sat down next to me.

"Harriet, what a surprise! So good to see you!"

I looked over and recognized Howard Levine. He had been my late stepfather Mort's partner in Mort's Mortuary and Crematorium. Since Mort had gone to his heavenly reward a few years ago, Howard was now the sole owner of the lucrative funeral-parlor chain.

I'd known him since my teen years, when Mom had married Mort, who'd set us up in the good life. Howard used to come over to our big new house most weekends to play cards with Mort and a bunch of other old geezers out by the pool.

I hadn't seen him since Mort's funeral. He was in good shape for a septuagenarian. He was slightly taller than me, trim and a natty dresser. He wore a well-cut navy suit with a crisp white shirt and a paisley tie. The white hair on the back of his bald head was neatly combed in place. Now there's something I've always respected: bald guys who just let their natural appearance be instead of doing those ridiculous comb-overs that fool nobody and only advertise the poor schmuck's low self-image.

"So what are you doing here?" Howard asked, gazing at me through his rimless glasses.

"Oh, looking into a possible connection on a case I'm working on," I said.

"Yes, that's right, your mother did tell me that you're a private eye now."

"Yes. By the way, I understand that you're doing the Reverend Botay's funeral tomorrow. I plan to come."

"Oh, yes. You knew her?"

I nodded.

"I didn't," he said, "but what a shame about her death." He paused a moment. "Say, I read that she was in the forefront of the gay-rights movement, and today the council is having a hearing on the same-sex marriage issue. Her murder wouldn't be the case you're investigating, would it?"

"Actually, yes."

"But I thought the killer had already been apprehended."

"Well, there are some who doubt his guilt. So I'm looking into it."

"Oh, that's wonderful. If the police suspect didn't do it, I'm sure you'll find out who did."

"Thanks for the vote of confidence. By the way, what time is the funeral?"

He frowned. "Oh, dear, I can't recall exactly. I've got a few scheduled for tomorrow. But I'm pretty sure it's at two."

"Okay, I'll be there. Now, what brings you here today?"

"Oh, a different matter altogether. You've heard of the city's proposal to renovate the bridge that spans the canal separating Boca from Deerfield Beach?"

"No, I haven't."

"Well, they want to make the bridge the gateway to Boca. A real eye-catching spectacle. The architectural plans call for adorning the new bridge with statues."

"Well, that sounds nice. They have that in all the European cities, and it's beautiful." I'd done some international travel in my Boca Babe days.

Now my excursions were strictly limited to my hog rides. Those didn't take me far, but it was as far as I need to go.

"No, you don't understand," Howard said. "These aren't statues of saints or knights. They're iguanas!"

I blinked. "What?"

"Yes, they want to put giant green iguana statues on the bridge."

"Why?"

"The city planners, a bunch of whippersnappers with BURP degrees—"

"Wait, what?" I interrupted.

"BURP—bachelor of urban and regional planning. These kids have been taking their lunch breaks on the banks of that canal and they've seen these live iguanas lying around there, sunning themselves. They get the bright idea that iguana statues would provide a great symbol of Boca."

"Well, that has possibilities," I said. "You know, there's a Saint Ignatius of Loyola, so why not a Saint Iguana of Lake Boca? Or how about a Knight of the Iguana?"

"Please, Harriet. This is no laughing matter. These proposed iguanas are totally tasteless. Completely kitschy. And you know my funeral home is located right by that bridge. Can you imagine grief-stricken mourners coming to pay their respects to their departed loved ones and being confronted with those iguanas? It would be a slap in their face! My business would plunge right into the canal!

"So that's why I'm here. The city council is taking public comments on the bridge proposal today, and I'm here to express my vehement opposition. In fact, you know, I'm sure your mother would fully agree with me on this. Surely she would not want the business that Mort—rest his soul—worked so hard to build to now be demeaned and ruined in this way."

"Yes, I'm sure Mort would be mortified," I said. "I'll mention it to her."

At that point the council members filed in and took their seats. The mayor, a fortyish man with slicked-back hair and sharp facial features, sat in the center.

"Ladies and gentlemen," he began, "we have numerous orders of business before us today. I'm sure you all have the agenda, so we'll go ahead and get started."

Actually, I didn't have the agenda, but I didn't really care. I knew what I was there for.

"Our first item of business is to receive public comments on the proposed same-sex marriage ordinance."

Great! Since my own agenda item was first, I wouldn't have to sit through the iguana-bridge issue and whatever else there was. As soon as the gay marriage hearing was done, I could leave and get on with the investigation.

The mayor continued, "Anyone who wishes to speak, please line up at the microphones at the front of the room. Each speaker will have three minutes."

They were already lined up, and the first was a boyish-looking guy with blond hair and a pointy goatee, wearing a white suit and white tie. He looked like a young version of Colonel Sanders of KFC fame. Once that image entered my mind, so did one of extra-crispy, all-white meat with mashed potatoes and a flaky biscuit. My mouth started salivating.

"Mr. Mayor and honorable members of the council," he began, "I am Pastor Fred Hollings of the Church of the Serpentine Redeemer."

What the hell was that? My indoctrination into the religious realm was becoming weirder and weirder.

The pastor went on, "I am here as the leader of the Christian Righteous Against Perverts."

Christian Righteous Against Perverts. I needed an easy way to remember that. Acronyms were always good mnemonic aids. So this one was…CRAP.

"We firmly believe that passage of this ordinance would seriously undermine the moral values of our community," the pastor said. "As you all know, the Holy Bible unequivocally condemns homosexuality. Homosexuals will suffer eternal damnation unless they repent and accept Jesus Christ as their savior from their satanic temptations. And, as you all know, the Bible defines marriage as between a man and a woman."

Hey, wait a minute. Wasn't it more like a man and multiple women?

"So passage of this ordinance would mean rejecting the Judeo-Christian principles that we all share. It will defile the state of holy matrimony. If homosexuals are allowed to marry, what's next? Man and child? Man and beast? I'm telling you, Mr. Mayor and honorable council members, if you pass this ordinance, Boca Raton will become Sodom. And it will all be on your heads. You will all be Sodomites. And you know what God did to them. He's already given Boca numerous warnings. First we had that anthrax incident right after 9/11. Then we've had four major hurricanes in the last two years. These are direct expressions of the Lord's displeasure, ladies and gentlemen. Boca will be wiped off the face of the earth. Just look at what happened to New Orleans, that den of iniquity with all its vice and sin and homosexuality."

"Your time is up," the mayor interrupted. "Thank you for your comments, sir."

Hollings sat down. Well, here was one hate-filled

human being. Certainly a potential suspect in the reverend's murder. I'd be having a little talk with him.

As the next speaker came up, visions of golden fried chicken floated in my mind's eye. Get a grip, I told myself. I had a job to do here. And daydreaming about chicken was not it.

The next speaker introduced himself as the Reverend Thomas Orlansky, representing the Christians for Human Enlightenment and Equal Rights.

Okay, another group name to remember. The acronym for this one was...CHEER.

"Mr. Mayor, honorable council members," he began, "with all due respect, Pastor Hollings has sadly and seriously misinterpreted biblical tenets. We cannot take the Bible as literal truth. It is an allegory open to interpretation as time evolves. If we took it literally, we would also be condoning ownership of women and children as property, capital punishment for petty theft, and many other outdated notions that civil society has rejected.

"And let us not forget that the Bible also tells us to love our neighbor as ourselves. The gay and

lesbian members of our community are our neighbors, and deserving of the same rights and privi-
leges as everyone else. Furthermore, there is no
evidence that gay unions contribute to moral
decline. Thank you for allowing me to speak, ladies
and gentlemen."

"Thank you, sir," said the mayor.

Okay, this guy was on the same side as the
Reverend Botay, so probably not a suspect in her
death. But who knew? I moved him to the bottom
of my list but didn't cross him off.

Several other speakers followed, all expressing
their support or opposition along the same lines as
the first two. As I listened, my mind wandered to
buttery soft biscuits, mashed potatoes and spicy
gravy. I added them all to my suspect list (the
speakers, not the biscuits, potatoes and gravy).

When an hour was up, the mayor said, "Those
are all the comments we can accept. Thank you all
for your input. Our next step on this issue will be
to obtain a recommendation from the council's
Citizens' Ethics Advisory Committee. And in that

vein, I ask for a moment of silence in memory of one of the Ethics Committee members, the Reverend LaVerne Botay, whose untimely passing has come as a shock to us all."

After the appointed moment, the mayor announced, "We will now move to our next agenda item, the renovation of the canal bridge. We are open to public comments. The same rules apply as for the previous speakers."

Howard rushed up to the microphone, but didn't make it before a short round woman in a lavender suit and sensible shoes, who introduced herself as Gertrude Klein, representing the citizens' group I Wanna Iguana.

I'd heard what I'd come for. I was outta there and on my way to catch a killer.

But not before a stop at the nearest KFC.

CHAPTER 6

Following a very satisfying, grease-filled lunch, I decided to pay a visit to Pastor Hollings, currently my prime suspect. I called information and got the address of the Church of the Serpentine Redeemer, then hopped on my hog and rode over.

As the bike got into gear, so did my thinking. Riding always freed up my mind. I reflected on my newfound knowledge that the Reverend Botay was a member of the Citizens' Ethics Advisory Committee, which was to make a recommendation on the same-sex marriage ordinance. Knowing that she would argue for the ordinance, potentially influencing the other committee members to make a recommendation in favor of it, strengthened the case for her having been killed by the antigay movement. I congratulated myself for being on the right track. Then I remembered that I hadn't put myself on that track, the Holy Rollers had.

I arrived at the church, which was located in a converted old supermarket. Inside, I was greeted by the ubiquitous Boca Babe wannabe receptionist. They inhabit every office in town, with their cheap fake hair, cheap fake nails and not-so-cheap fake boobs. The wannabes are in search of husbands to magically transform them from Boca Babe imitations into the real thing. The Cinderella dream is alive and well in Boca. Apparently, even houses of worship aren't exempt from the flesh peddling.

The receptionist was busy checking her makeup in a compact mirror, practicing to be a future Boca Babe. Mirror-gazing is a favorite pastime of theirs. In fact, suburban legend has it that the way a guy can tell if a Boca Babe has had an orgasm during sex is if she drops her compact.

I asked the woman for Hollings. Looking aggrieved, she placed the compact in her desk drawer and wearily escorted me through a large open space filled with plastic chairs facing a podium. Marks left by the former supermarket aisles were still visible on the floor, and I swore a smell of fish still hung in the air.

We reached the back of the building. Ms. Babe Wannabe knocked on a door. Upon hearing a *yes* from within, she pushed it open, allowing me to enter.

Now, I've seen some shocking shit in my life, but what I saw here had to be near the top of the pile. The pastor sat behind his desk, with four live snakes crawling all over him. A fifth humongous one was curled up on top of the desk.

I backed out of the doorway in revulsion.

"Fear not, young lady," Hollings said.

Hey, what was he doing calling me young? He looked as if he'd just barely escaped adolescence.

"I see you're unfamiliar with our spiritual practices," he said. "Let me fill you in. The Holy Book tells us that those who believe in Jesus Christ will not fear serpents nor be harmed by them. So handling these snakes is a worshipper's demonstration of faith. These serpents are an integral part of our services."

"Oh," I said. "I thought the reason they didn't bite you was out of professional courtesy."

"Well, it's obvious you are not one of the faithful," he replied. "So I'll put these away to ease your infidel discomfort."

He unwound the smaller ones.

"Okay, Lucy, Ricardo, Fred, Ethel, come on. Time to rest for a bit."

He placed them into four large glass aquariums lined up along the wall behind him.

"Now, Monty, you, too."

He picked up the big one off the desk and placed it in an aquarium of its own.

"Don't tell me," I said. "Monty Python?"

"Why, yes," he replied.

This guy watched way too much oldies TV.

"Now, please come in, sit down," Hollings said. "You are out of harm's way. For the time being, anyway. Just remember, it's your disconnection from the Lord that's the cause of all your life's miseries."

Oh, yeah, like I really came here for an admonishing sermon.

I took one of the chairs in front of his desk. Now that the python was gone, I noticed two books lying there: *Catholic Devotions for Dummies* and *Islamic Ideology for Idiots*. Well, those appellations certainly seemed appropriate for him.

He saw me gazing at the books and remarked, "In our holy war for righteousness, we must have knowledge of the enemy, right?"

"Uh, yeah, right." What would he read next? *Jewish Law for Lamebrains*? Maybe he could write his own: *Fundamentalist Foundations for Fools*.

"Now, what can I do for you?" he asked.

I introduced myself, explained that I was investigating the Reverend Botay's murder, and that I wondered if he wouldn't mind answering a few questions.

"Why, certainly. What a dreadful tragedy. I heard it on the news yesterday. Although the reverend and I certainly didn't see eye to eye on many matters of Christian orthodoxy, in the end one must put aside one's differences and join in the spirit of fellowship, mustn't one? I'm ashamed of not having done so before it was too late. Well, none of us is perfect. We are all sinners, aren't we? But through our Lord Jesus Christ's death and resurrection, we can all be saved."

Okay, enough already with the preaching. Jeez, would I be dogged by this dogmatism throughout this whole doggone investigation?

"So exactly how can I help you?" he asked.

"Well, Pastor, as you just said yourself, you and the reverend were on opposing sides of many issues. I know this same-sex marriage one has been particularly contentious. In fact, I've been told the reverend had received death threats over this. Would you know of anyone in your camp who may have wished her harm?"

"Most certainly not! As I said, indeed we are all sinners, but no one from the Christian Righteous Against Perverts would ever dream of committing murder. Of course, it's prohibited by the Ten Commandments, and we take those with the utmost seriousness."

Okay, how was it that we were all sinners, but

some sins were worse than others? Why was being gay a greater sin than calling someone a pervert?

This was pissing me off. I wasn't going to sit here and take this CRAP. I went on the offensive.

"Pastor, where were you on Sunday afternoon around two o'clock?" I asked.

"Why, right here. Our services ended around noon, then I mingled with my flock, and after they all left I came here into my office to unwind myself and the snakes."

"Is there anyone who can verify your where-abouts?"

"No one but the serpents." He nodded toward the beasts behind him.

Well, hell. There was no incriminating information here. The guy didn't have a confirmable alibi, but by the same token, there was nothing pointing to his involvement.

"Well, thanks for your time," I said and rose to leave.

"Just remember, young lady, we are here to spread the Good News. All you need do is turn your life over to the Lord Jesus, repent your sins, and receive eternal salvation and serpentine redemption."

"Yeah, I'll consider that," I said. As if. I'd rather be with Satan than with those vipers.

CHAPTER 7

The next morning I had to go to the grocery store to buy something for the potluck that would follow the reverend's funeral that afternoon. I fretted about what to bring. As a former Boca Babe, my cooking skills didn't amount to a hill of beans. Cooking just wasn't part of the job description, and my recovery process hadn't yet led me to change my ways on that. So I figured I'd just grab something at the deli counter.

Since I was going into town early, I also decided to go work out at Lior's Krav Maga studio before going on to the funeral. One good thing was I wouldn't have to change from my street clothes, which were always all black, into funeral attire. As a woman in black, I was always prepared for the worst. That way the worst would never get the best of me.

I rode my dual modes of transportation into town. I managed to park the hog in the Publix grocery parking lot without incident. This is always a minor miracle because South Florida parking lots are literally jammed with disoriented seniors who seriously should not be behind the wheel of a lethal weapon.

Inside the store, I grabbed a large container of coleslaw and considered my duty fulfilled. I headed straight for the express checkout, deftly sidestepping the usual multitude of oblivious customers who blocked the aisles with their carts, moved at the speed of Arctic glaciers and made sudden turns or backups without warning. I seriously think that Publix should have one-way aisles with traffic lights and crossing guards. I decided to take that up with the management in the near future.

The Drag Angel cashier was on duty at the cash register. I call her that in my mind because her extreme makeup makes her look like a drag queen, and her unfailing words of kindness to customers make her an angel. Today her bouffant blond hair ballooned out a good eight inches from her head, her plucked-out eyebrows were carefully drawn on with brown pencil, and her sky-blue eye shadow sparkled with flecks of silver.

"Sweetie, you look lovely today," she said to me.

See what I mean? I looked the same as every other day, but she had something nice to say nonetheless.

"Thank you," I said. "How are you doing?"

"Grateful to be alive. You know, sweetie, I'm at the age now where all my friends are depressed, demented or dead. But I'm happy, I've still got my mind, and I'm still kicking. So I got no complaints."

"With that attitude, I'm sure you'll be around for a good long time," I said.

I paid for my coleslaw and headed for the door. When I stepped outside, I saw a bunch of seniors gazing up at the sky.

"What the heck is that?" one asked.

"Looks like he's writing something," another one said.

I looked up. A skywriter was flying overhead. The pilot had spelled out the letters *LOV* with the plane's contrails.

I'd seen this plane fly over Boca many times. The pilot always wrote the same message: JESUS LOVES YOU. The trouble was, by the time he got to the second word, the first one had faded out, and when he got to the third, the second one was gone. So anyone who happened to look up at any one time would always see only part of the message, never the whole thing. Either you had to have a lot of patience to watch it all from beginning to end, or you needed to catch it in different stages at different times, as I had. I quickly explained this to the gathered seniors, who rapidly dispersed, grumbling, inasmuch as this part of town was heavily populated with Jewish residents.

As I rode over to Lior's fitness studio, I started thinking about that skywriter and my case. Just as with that message in the sky, if I was to make sense of this case I'd need to see the whole picture, not just the pieces. And I hoped that the investigative trails I followed, unlike the contrails of that plane, wouldn't disappear into thin air, leaving me without a clue.

When I arrived at the studio for a twelve o'clock class, no other participants were in sight. The place was empty.

"Hello?" I called.

Lior stepped out of a back room. His six-foot-three, broad-shouldered frame nearly took up the doorway. He wore a pair of faded jeans and a blue silk shirt unbuttoned at the collar. A lock of black hair hung down over one of his dark eyes. He grinned as he pushed it off his face.

Damn, he looked good. I felt a stir between my legs. Stop it, I commanded myself. I'd come to work out, not make out.

"Well, what a pleasant surprise," he said in his slightly accented (and yes, sexy) voice. "You dropped in just to see me?"

What an ego! This guy was so cocksure of himself. And I was sure I wanted his co— Stop it, stop it, I repeated to myself. Get a grip.

"No," I snapped. "I didn't come to see you. I'm here for the twelve o'clock class. Where is everybody?"

"Didn't you get the monthly newsletter? That

class is now on Tuesdays and Fridays, not Mondays and Wednesdays."

Well, shit. I had gotten a little behind on opening my personal mail.

"Okay, I guess I'll come back tomorrow," I said.

"Wait. It would be a shame for you to have come all the way over here for nothing. Why don't we have a one-on-one?"

"Excuse me? We've gotten together twice—don't you even dare call those dates—and you expect me to jump your bones? You can take that idea and—"

"Don't flatter yourself, Horowitz," he said. But there was a gleam in his eyes. "I wasn't talking about doing *it*. I'm talking about doing *combat*. You know, what you came here for?"

"Oh. Yeah, sure. I'll go one-on-one with you. Anytime, anyplace." Man, why did I have to make such a fool of myself?

"Here and now," he said. "Go change."

I went into the women's locker room and put on my scrappy old gym clothes. I emerged ready for major battle.

Lior had changed, too, into black sweats. We took our places on the mat, facing each other. Lior took the role of attacker and I the defender. He started with a kick aimed at my solar plexus. I caught his foot in my hands and pushed it upward, flipping him onto his back. Before I could release his foot he grabbed my arms, pulling me down on top of him.

We were face-to-face, chest-to-chest, hip-to-hip. He felt hard…all over. Keeping his eyes on mine, he hooked his right leg over my left and simultaneously pushed my right shoulder, flipping me over so he was now on top.

"I think I liked it better the other way," he said.

"Glad you enjoyed it, because it's not gonna happen again."

He had my arms pinned down with his hands, and his body weight had me immobilized. Now, Krav Maga has no rules. Anything goes in the interest of self-defense. Having been a practitioner for several years, this principle was deeply ingrained in me, so I had no misgivings about doing whatever it took to restore my dominance in the situation.

You're supposed to use whatever resources you have at hand. And in this case, one of my resources was the knowledge that Lior had the hots for me. So I raised my head and kissed him. His lips were soft and responsive. I almost forgot why I'd made this move. Self-defense, I reminded myself. That's all this is about. As the kiss lingered, his grip loosened. I slid my arms down until I intertwined my fingers with his, then I snapped back his wrists in one quick move. He groaned in pain and rolled off me.

We went on like this for a half hour until we were both breathing hard and dripping with sweat. We lay down next to each other on our backs, in the recovery phase.

A few minutes later, when our breathing had slowed, Lior said, "That was great." He squeezed my hand, then rolled over and got up. I watched him go to the restroom and shut the door. Shortly thereafter I heard the toilet flush. Damn if this whole thing wasn't identical to a postcoital scenario.

I had to get out, quick. When he came out of the restroom I was already heading for the locker room.

"Don't you want to stay and, I don't know, talk? Maybe have a drink of Red Bull to revive?"

Talk about bull. What did he think this was—a relationship? All it was was se…self-defense, no more.

"No, I've got things to do. Thanks for the se…session."

"A little commitment-phobic, Horowitz?" he said to my retreating back. "No problem. When it comes to getting what I want, I'm very patient. And persistent."

There he went with that cockiness again. I wasn't going to put up with this egomaniac. I entered the locker room and slammed the door behind me. I showered and changed.

When I came out, Lior's office door was closed and he wasn't in sight. Perfect. No goodbye necessary.

It was time to head over to the reverend's funeral. When I got to the mortuary, the parking lot was empty. Strange. Why was this happening to me twice in one day? Howard had said the funeral was at two, hadn't he? I looked at my watch. It was twenty till. I guess I was early. I went in to wait.

Inside, there was nobody in sight. I sat down in the antechamber. The side table held issues of *Mortuary Management* and *Funeral Monitor*. I idly leafed through them. Now, I suppose funeral directors might enjoy spending their evenings sitting by the fireplace, sipping sherry and reading about the latest embalming techniques or negotiations with grave diggers' unions. But anyone else would die of boredom. I put the journals back and sat there, feeling restless. My mind kept wandering back to my encounter with Lior. To the feel of his body on mine, his lips on mine.

Oh, this was ridiculous. I had to distract myself. I got up to walk around. I knew the mortuary well since Mort occasionally had let me and my adolescent friends hang out there for thrills.

I wandered into the display room, checking out the variety of coffins and urns available. This being Boca, containers for the dead tended toward the over-the-top. You could get an actual sarcophagus from ancient Rome or an urn from ancient Greece. You could get a coffin carved with a custom epitaph, like *Here Lie I, an Atheist, All Dressed Up* with *No Place to Go*, or *Gone Away, Owing More than I Could Pay.*

I strolled out of there and into the consultation room. I sat down at the desk and looked through the three-ring binder that described various kinds of services and arrangements. I swear this was just like a party planner's portfolio, which I'd seen plenty of as a Boca Babe. As with birthdays, graduations, weddings and such, the purpose of funerals in Boca was to outdo your friends and neighbors. You wanted an event that people would talk about for years to come.

There was the football fanatic whose funeral had featured a performance by the entire Miami Dolphins cheerleading squad. There was the developer who'd had custom-made Monopoly games given to all his mourners as party favors. The game board was made of bronze; the tokens were silver; the houses were gold; the hotels were platinum; and the money was real. And then there was the plastic surgeon whose send-off included a lottery for a free boob job by his business partner.

I went into the next room. It held an open casket surrounded by flowers. I knew what that meant: there was a body inside. It couldn't be the Reverend Botay. Since her service was about to begin, her casket would be in the building's chapel.

Okay, I'll admit I have a morbid curiosity. I strolled over to see if I knew the deceased, and more importantly, to see how good a job the makeup artist had done.

I got to the edge, but before I could get a look, I was suddenly grabbed from behind.

A voice whispered in my ear, "This is what you get for snooping. This thing is going into the cremation oven. Burn, baby, burn!"

Hey, weren't those the lyrics from "Disco Inferno"? Was this some kind of sick joke? Guess not.

Just as I started to make a Krav Maga move to escape, my attacker shoved my torso into the coffin facedown, lifted my legs, threw them in over the side and slammed the lid shut.

I was trapped—on top of a corpse!

CHAPTER 8

I was cheek to cheek with the corpse. Its face was cold and waxen. The two of us were stuffed into this box built for one. I couldn't move an inch. My face was smashed into the pillow on which the corpse's head rested. I screamed, but the noise was totally muffled by the pillow. I could hardly breathe. And it was pitch-black in there. Claustrophobic panic seized me to my very core.

Suddenly, I felt the coffin being wheeled. Then I heard a voice. Female.

"Lapidus, Lapidus, my darling, how will I go on without you?" she wailed.

Oh, my God. I recognized the voice, and the identity of the corpse.

The voice belonged to Brigitta Larsen O'Malley,

a queen bee Boca Babe. We were the same age and she'd been a "friend" back in the day. And the corpse was that of her eighty-something husband, Lapidus O'Malley.

Holy shit! I was really freaked now. If lying on top of a corpse wasn't bad enough, lying on top of Lapidus O'Malley was just too much to bear.

Lapidus had been a senior partner in my former husband's law firm, which raked in millions defending pharmaceutical companies, auto manufacturers, toy makers and the like against the little people who'd been injured or killed by the corporations' utter disregard for human welfare. The firm's tactics consisted of intimidation and delay until the plaintiffs were totally worn down and gave up. And if that didn't work, there was always their favorite strategy: the nuts 'n' sluts defense. You know the one, where every female plaintiff or witness is either a nut or a slut, or, preferably, both. Lapidus was the major force behind it all, and thus lower than a snake's belly.

I just couldn't take this. I began to choke and gag.

Then I heard another voice—Howard's!

"Mrs. O'Malley," he said. "You've said your final farewells. Please don't deepen your grief now. It would be best if you stepped out. One of my assistants will be happy to sit with you. We really advise against family members accompanying the deceased in this final journey."

"Yes, all right," Brigitta sobbed.

I couldn't catch my breath to scream. I struggled to move my arms and legs to beat on the coffin walls, but there was no space to move. I was immobilized.

I heard footsteps receding, then returning.

Yet another voice came. Male this time.

"Okay, let's go ahead and wheel it into the oven."

This was it. I was about to die. A strange sense of calm came over me. The fear was gone.

Then I heard Howard again.

"Wait!" he said. "This thing isn't going in. That family is so cheap, they only rented this fancy casket to impress the gatherers at the service. We've got to take him out, put him in a cardboard box, then that's what goes in the oven."

Suddenly the coffin lid swung open. As I pushed myself up, I closed my eyes against the blinding light and gasped for air.

Howard and the other guy screamed.

"Oh, my God," Howard yelled. "Harriet! How did you get in there?"

"Are you all right? Let me help you out," the other guy said.

I felt his arms on me and climbed out of the coffin, my eyes still closed. I was led to a chair and told to sit. I did and lowered my head between my knees. When my breathing became normal, I slowly opened my eyes and sat up.

Howard and the other guy were staring at me, their faces pale and sickly.

"Oh, jeez," I said. "Sit down, you two. You look like you're in worse shape than I am."

They took a couple chairs.

I quickly explained what had happened.

"Oh, this is dreadful, just dreadful," Howard moaned, wringing his hands. "Who could have done such a thing?"

"I don't know," I said. "Did you see anyone around?"

They both shook their heads.

"It's obviously someone who thought this coffin was going into the oven," I said. "They wanted me dead. So for one thing, it couldn't be O'Malley's family, since they knew this casket was only a rental. Anyway, Brigitta doesn't have anything against me, that I know of. We're not friends anymore, but we're not enemies, either. Our lives just went in different directions."

Killing your husband tends to have that effect.

"I think it's connected to the case I'm working on, the Reverend Botay's murder," I continued. "What's the deal with her funeral, anyway? You told me it was at two. That's why I came here."

"Oh, dear," Howard moaned again. "Is that what I said? I must have misspoken. It's at three."

I looked at my watch. It was three now.

"Well, let's not keep the mourners waiting," I said. "Let's get the show on the road."

We all rose and stepped to the door.

"Oh, and one more thing," I said, turning back to them. "Not a word about this to anyone. The assailant could be one of the attendees. It's certainly well-known that killers often show up at the victim's funeral."

Or was that only in the movies? Whatever. That wasn't my main concern, actually. My mother was.

"I don't want my mother to hear a thing about this," I said. "She'd order me to get out of the P.I. business immediately, and if I didn't, she'd kill me herself."

CHAPTER 9

The chapel was packed. I took one of the few remaining seats as Howard and his assistant went to the front to begin the proceedings. At a quick glance I saw that all the attendees from the aborted wedding were there, including the contessa, Mom and Leonard, and the Holy Rollers, in drag, including Trey—Honey du Mellon—who was out of jail on bond.

At a nod from Howard, the Rollers rose, proceeded to the front and started the service by singing, "Will the Circle Be Unbroken." Following that there was not a dry eye in the house. Then Lupe gave the eulogy, recounting the reverend's life, challenges and achievements and reminding the mourners to carry on her mission.

Numerous speakers followed, each sharing warm personal recollections of the deceased. The ceremony closed with a glorious rendition of "When the Saints Go Marching In" by the Rollers, leaving everyone in a more uplifted mood. Howard informed the gathering that the reverend's body would be cremated and her ashes spread at sea, according to her wishes, which she had expressed from time to time to various church members.

Then directions to Lupe's house were passed around and we all rose to depart. The Rollers and I decided to ride over on our hogs as a group. After the Rollers had changed into their street clothes, we took off.

The reverberation produced by six hogs together created a formidable, yet melodious sound. In its own way, it was music, like an echo of the Rollers' harmony. I'd always been a lone rider, so this experience of group unity was new and unexpectedly affecting.

Upon our arrival at Lupe's, each of us unloaded

our potluck contributions from our saddlebags
and went in.

Lupe's house was a gorgeous Bahamian-style
cottage: square, wooden, with a tin roof, large
shutters and a wraparound porch. Outside, a flower
garden flourished. The inside was lavishly and
lovingly decorated with indigenous art from
Mexico and Central America.

Many of the gatherers were already there, congre-
gating in small groups while eating off paper plates.
The large, carved wood dining-room table overflowed
with food. I squeezed my container of coleslaw onto
the table, hoping no one would notice me and my
paltry offering. Hey, at least I took off the price sticker.

I filled a plate with actual cooked food and looked
around. I spotted my mother talking with Howard.
I saw Leonard sitting alone so I went to join him.

"Harriet, please sit down," he invited, patting
the couch cushion next to him.

I did, and we chatted a bit about the tragedy, the
touching and thoroughly fitting funeral service and
how my mother was holding up. Then Leonard

launched into his favorite topic, the Cold War. I liked the guy and was even starting to be cool with this weird fixation he had. I realized that, as a retired spook, the Cold War represented his glory days, and I couldn't deny him the pleasure of recounting his adventures. He waxed poetic about infiltrating the Russkies, setting bugs in the tunnel under the Berlin Wall, and on and on.

Then my mother joined us. We squeezed over on the couch and she sat on Leonard's other side.

"Harriet," she said, "I was just speaking with Howard. He was telling me about the city's awful plans to put iguanas on the bridge right by Mort's."

"Oh, yes, I know. I meant to tell you about it. I happened to see Howard yesterday, and he told me."

"Well, this is just dreadful. We can't allow this to happen. Poor Mort would flip in his grave. I told Howard I would do whatever I could to help him defeat this proposal. In fact, I'm going to start by passing around a petition in the neighborhood. You'll help me, Leonard, won't you?"

"Of course, sweetheart."

What a gracious man. Not every guy would be so willing to act on behalf of his love's former husband.

"Good idea, Mom," I said. "Doing something active might help you get over your grief."

She sighed. "Yes. But, my dears, I am so overwrought," she said, playing drama queen again. Leonard patted her hand.

"I just can't understand who would do such a thing to that wonderful woman," she went on. "Harriet, you must find whoever committed this heinous act." Apparently she'd heard by now that I was on the case.

"I intend to," I said.

"I know the Holy Rollers think Trey was framed," she said. "Maybe it was by someone whom he had sentenced in his court and who held a grudge."

"Could be," I said. "I'll look into that possibility."

"Or maybe it was someone who had an upcoming trial scheduled in Trey's court, and got him out of the way so they could get a more lenient judge."

"Yeah. I'll look into that one, too."

Shit, why hadn't I thought of these things

myself? I was the P.I. here, not Mom. Irritated, I made my excuses to Mom and Leonard and went to talk to the Holy Rollers, who were standing out on the porch.

Trey looked as if he'd lost ten pounds and aged ten years during his two days in jail. He was slightly taller than me, and had been of medium build, but now looked gaunt. He thanked me profusely for taking on his case. I decided to swallow my pride and follow up on Mom's ideas.

"Trey," I asked, "do you think anyone other than the gay-marriage protesters could have framed you?"

"Oh, Harriet, I've thought and thought about that endlessly. I've been on the bench for fifteen years. Naturally, many of the defendants who came before me were unhappy, to say the least, with my judicial decisions. So it could be any one of them. But I think there's only one likely candidate worth some scrutiny."

"Who?" I asked eagerly.

"Guy named Lucas Morse. He's a young punk, a leader of a small-time local white supremacist group calling themselves the Loyal Brotherhood of Aryans. He was coming up to trial in a couple weeks on hate-crime charges. He'd been caught in flagrante delicto—"

"Wait, excuse me, fragrant delectable what?" I interrupted. I seemed to be doing that a lot lately. But give me a break. I'm a recovering Babe. The knowledge required for that job is not particularly broad. But as in any kind of recovery, one of the steps is admitting your shortcomings to your fellow human beings. So that's what I was doing.

"Oh, I'm sorry. I lapsed into legalese. What I mean is, he was caught red-handed painting swastikas on the Temple Beth Boca. You can imagine he wasn't pleased with coming before a black judge."

"Yes, I can imagine. Where would I find this dirtball?"

"I don't know where he lives or works. Try the D.A.'s office. Tell them I referred you and they'll give you the information."

"On it," I said.

I decided to call it a day, so I went around and

said my goodbyes to everyone. Then I went out, donned my helmet and leathers, straddled my hog, fired it up and headed for home.

It was dark by the time I got there. I sat down on the porch with my Hennessy and pondered the day's events. As I sat there staring into the night, Lana's snout emerged from the swamp.

"Who the hell shoved me into that coffin?" I asked her.

"Think about everyone you've seen or talked to since you took the case," she suggested.

"Okay. On Monday I was hired by the Rollers. Wait. Could one of *them* have set up Honey? Could there be a Judas among them?"

"Think, girl!" Lana replied. "They were all at the altar before and after Honey got there and before you found the body. Assuming that Honey was not the killer, then the murder must have happened after Honey left the clothes-changing room. So the Rollers' whereabouts at the time of the murder are accounted for. Same with all the wedding guests. They were all seated well before

Honey got there, and none of them left afterward."

"Well, thank God for that. I won't have to interview a hundred potential suspects. Okay…so then on Monday I had lunch with Lupe and she gave me names of the church board members. Then I called those people. So they know I'm on the case. It could be one of them."

"Yep. Check 'em out."

"Right. Now, yesterday I went to the council meeting. I didn't say anything to anyone there about being on the case."

"Except Howard."

"Yeah. But whoever shoved me in the coffin meant for me to burn. He or she thought that coffin was going into the oven. But Howard knew it wasn't. So it couldn't be him."

"I guess not," Lana conceded with a swish of her tail.

"Then yesterday afternoon I went to see Hollings. Our encounter was fairly antagonistic. He creeps me out with those snakes, and I guess I creep him out with my…well, my existence. So I'd have to say he's the most likely candidate. He must have figured I was likely to attend the reverend's funeral. So he could have been waiting there for me. Maybe he went to O'Malley's funeral first and learned that O'Malley was going to be cremated and then got the idea of how to do me in. Or he could have had an accomplice do it."

"But how would he know you'd be in the back room of the funeral home?"

"Shit, I don't know. Maybe he planned to lure me back there somehow and just got lucky that I showed up on my own."

"Well, I'll have to agree with you," she said. "He's still the prime suspect. Watch your back."

"I'll watch mine if you'll watch yours."

"Very funny. You know damn well I can only see sideways and I don't have a neck to turn my head around."

"Well, that doesn't seem to have hurt you any. Aren't you guys the oldest living reptiles on earth?"

"Indeed we are." She flashed her teeth. Was that

a gator grin? "We've seen the dinosaurs come and go, seen all the predecessors of Homo sapiens come and go, and I hate to tell you…."

"Yeah, yeah, you'll still be here when we're gone. You and the cockroaches. That's real nice, Lana."

"Well, there's no need to get huffy," she said.

"Fine, whatever. Now look, I don't know what more to do about Hollings at this point. I think my next move should be to follow up on this Lucas Morse scumbag that Trey talked about. But how the hell will I get to him? A direct confrontation probably won't get me anywhere. After all, look where it got me with Hollings. I think this calls for undercover work. But how?"

"I have an idea," Lana said. "Remember when you stepped out of the church after the murder and there was half the population of Boca thinking this was a TV show and looking to have their brush with fame?"

"Yeah," I said.

"And remember how you thought reality was stranger than fiction in Boca?"

"Yeah."

"Well, think about that some more," she commanded. Then she disappeared into the swamp.

What the hell was she talking about? She wasn't
usually this cryptic. But she was always right, so I
had to work with what she'd given me.

"TV, fame, reality," I repeated to myself over
and over. Finally it clicked: reality TV. That was
my answer to getting inside the Loyal Brotherhood
of Assholes.

CHAPTER 10

The next morning I went to the office and called the D.A. After I dropped Judge Harrison's name, he readily gave me Lucas Morse's address and phone number. Then, knowing that every hate group in America has a Web site to promote their vileness and recruit vulnerable youngsters, I looked up the Loyal Brotherhood of Aryans. Sure enough, they had a site and it was full of the usual revolting bullshit.

Now, even though I don't watch TV, I do read the newspaper occasionally, which inevitably has an article about one of those asinine reality shows. So I was familiar with the phenomenon. How could you not be? Those programs proliferated like weeds. Or parasites, sucking the lifeblood out of their viewers. Would someone please explain to me why anyone would sit on their ass watching somebody else's mind-numbing life instead of living their own?

Anyway, I picked up the phone and called Morse.

"Yeah?" a voice demanded.

"Lucas Morse?" I asked.

"Yeah, what's it to you?"

"My name is Har…uh, Hailey Holloway. I'm a locally based television producer from Hollywood."

"Hollywood, Florida, that pit of old freeloaders who should die already instead of draining our tax dollars?"

That Lucas, what a guy.

"No, sir, Hollywood, California."

That gave him pause.

"Sir, we are developing a new reality show called *American Patriot*. It's about concerned citizens striving to preserve the American way of life. I'm scouting for possible stars for the show. I came across your group's Web site and thought that you're just the kind of upstanding Americans that we want to showcase."

"Oh, yeah?" Now I had perked his interest.

"Absolutely. Sir, if you were on this show you and your group would get national exposure. It would be an unprecedented opportunity to spread your important message to the American people."

"So what do you want?"

"Well, I'd like to come and observe your group in action. If it looks like you're as perfect for the show as I think you are, I'll pull for you with my boss."

He was silent for a few moments. Then he bit.

"Yeah, okay. We're meeting at midnight tonight at the old sugar mill out on Hooker Highway. You know where that is?"

I knew. Hooker Highway was another one of those "Only in South Florida" phenomena.

"Yeah. And by the way, it's okay if I bring a video camera, right? I'll need it to take footage back to my executive producer to pitch your group for the show."

"Sure, I'm cool with that."

I knew it. He couldn't resist the lure of fame. Now *that*'s the American way.

"Great, I'll see you tonight," I said and hung up with a smug smile.

Then, reminding myself that I still needed to keep an open mind about all possibilities in the case, I decided to delve further into the reverend's life. Lupe had mentioned that the church had received a large monetary donation just before the reverend's murder. I wondered if there could be any connection there.

I could call the church board members I'd talked to before and see if they had any thoughts about that. But I figured I'd best lie low with them. If it was one of them who had pushed me into that coffin, maybe they'd think that they'd at least scared me off the case.

So instead, I looked up the donor, Dennis Pearlman, and called him at his office. Since he was the owner of a major company, he had myriad minions blocking access to him. But knowing what a publicity hound he was, once I merely stated that I was calling about his charitable activities, I was immediately scheduled for an appointment that afternoon.

I had a few hours to spare, so I worked on another case. This one was for a wealthy elderly widow who'd been scammed out of nearly a hundred grand by a con operation called Heaven, Inc., which promised a connection via a psychic medium to said location. After forking over the bucks in a series of enticements to communicate with her late spouse, she'd finally wised up. Since he wasn't answering, she'd decided that she'd been calling the wrong place all along, and he must be in hell instead of heaven. She figured Heaven, Inc. should have given her that information right off the bat, so she'd come to me to take them down. As with almost all my clients, she didn't go directly to the police since she didn't want the public embarrassment that comes with being a con victim. So I acted as a medium of a different sort.

For the past few weeks I'd been making calls to Heaven, posing variously as a bereaved daughter wanting to make amends with her departed mother, a terminally ill woman wanting to know her fate, a scorned woman wanting her guardian angel to tell her whether her lover would return and so on. Each time I was told that for additional payments, all would be revealed.

Today it was bound to be no different. I picked up the phone, turned on the built-in recorder and dialed 1-800-1-HEAVEN. I sat back as I listened to the recording on the other end.

"Thank you for calling Heaven, Inc. Please listen carefully to the following options, as our menu has changed. For our Master Medium, press one. For our Medium Assistant, press two. For our Medium Intern, press three…"

I pondered whether to go for the large medium, the medium medium, or the small medium. I decided to go straight to the top. I pressed one.

"We're sorry," the recording said, "The Master is unavailable to take your call. To return to the main menu, press one."

I went back and tried the intern. He was in.

I stuck a piece of chewing gum in my mouth and adopted a Queens accent.

"Yo, small fry? Listen, I think I met my future ex-husband today. He is one fine-lookin' specimen, but there's those little warning signs of danger ahead, you know what I'm sayin'? So what I want to know is, how much will I get out of homeboy in the divorce?"

"My child, you've called the right place," Small Fry replied. "Heaven does have the answer. You need only seek and it shall be revealed. However, I'm going to have to consult with the Master on this one and you know his time is valuable. But just for today, we have a special offer of only $99.99. But that's only good today so you need to act now. With this special offer, I'll bring up your case at our next leadership team meeting. I'm sure you don't want to pass up this great value. I'll take your credit-card number now."

That was the point where I did my standard sign-off, "I'll have to think about that, thanks," and hung up.

I decided I now had accumulated sufficient evidence to slam the scam, so I wrote my final report to the client with a CC to the police. They could now get an arrest warrant based on my evidence, rather than my client's, leaving her dignity intact.

As I was heading out to grab some lunch, the phone rang.

"Harriet? It's Gitta."

Who? Oh. Oh, my God. The recently widowed Brigitta Larsen O'Malley. What was she doing calling me? None of my former Babe "friends" had acknowledged my existence since I'd bumped off Bruce.

"Uh, hi, Gitta," I said.

"Sweetie, I heard what happened at Mort's," she said. Her voice was babyish, like Melanie Griffith's. She'd always spoken that way, and it had always grated on me. "You were locked in the casket with my darling Lapidus?"

"Well, yes, but I wouldn't call him dar… Oh, never mind."

"I am so horrified, sweetie. Look, can we get together?"

Get together? After four years of exile? True, my exile was self-imposed. And the shunning… Well, I guess it went both ways.

"Yeah, I guess we can get together," I said.

"What are you doing now?"

Now? "I was just heading out for some lunch."

"Would you mind if I joined you?"

Jeez. She was sounding desperate. Why didn't she just go hang out with her Babe buddies?

Then it struck me. With her husband dead, she was no longer a Babe. Just like that. The rules are simple: if you aren't owned by a man, with a huge stone on your finger to weigh you down, then you're not a Babe.

"Uh, okay," I said. "Yeah, you can join me. I'm going to Saul's Deli."

There was a pause, during which I imagined her turning up her nose. Saul's was just down the street from my office, far removed from Babe territory, geographically and gastronomically.

"Saul's?" she asked. "Sweetie, how about Chez Celine? Or Antoine's?"

"I'm going to Saul's," I repeated.

After another pause, she said, "Okay, I'll meet you there in twenty minutes."

"Fine," I said.

I walked to Saul's and took my usual seat by the window. While I waited for Gitta, I munched on pretzels and sipped a Corona with lime.

When Brigitta Larsen O'Malley came in, all eyes turned to her. And no wonder. Babes were rarely seen in this part of town. And Gitta had been Boca's reigning Babe. She was Danish with a figure and features to match. Tall, lithe, blonde and blue-eyed. In her early twenties, she'd been a Miss Universe runner-up. Now, over two decades later, she hadn't lost her beauty-queen looks. In the intervening time, she'd married Lapidus, borne his third set of children and, last I'd heard, had become an aerobics instructor at Boca's poshest athletic club.

I waved and she came over to my table. She started to give me the cheek-to-cheek air kiss that is the standard Babe greeting, but I backed off.

"Sorry, Gitta, I don't do affectations anymore. Have a seat."

She sat. Up close, she didn't look quite as good as she had from afar.

"I'm so sorry about…about Lapidus," I lied.

And then I choked on a pretzel.

I gasped for air. I coughed. I wheezed. I tried to swallow. The damn thing wasn't moving.

Son of a bitch! I was going to suffocate over Lapidus O'Malley after all.

CHAPTER 11

Gitta got up, rushed to my side and started hitting my back. I took a big gulp of Corona. Then, finally, I took a big gulp of air.

I don't know which saved me, Brigitta or beer. Whichever, I was free of Lapidus's eerie hold on me from beyond.

"Are you all right, sweetie?" Gitta asked.

"Yeah. I'm fine now. Thanks."

She sat back down and looked at me with concern. Her face was beautifully made up, as all Babes' are, but her eyes were bloodshot. I didn't know if that was from crying over Lapidus or from the coke habit I knew she had.

"Sweetie, thank you for seeing me," she said. "I

wanted to apologize about what happened at the funeral home."

"No apology necessary. It wasn't your fault."

"Howard said someone pushed you into the casket deliberately?"

"Yes."

"Do you have any idea who it was?"

"No."

That's all I intended to say on that subject. If she was even remotely connected to this thing, I certainly wasn't going to give her the slightest hint that I might be on the perp's trail. That would only invite another attempt on my life.

"So, why don't we order?" I asked. "I'm having pastrami on rye."

"Oh. Yes. Okay." She perused the menu. And perused.

Finally I said, "This place doesn't have your finger sandwiches, your Waldorf salads, or your carrot soup."

"Yes, okay." She sighed and ordered a large house salad with no dressing and some bottled water. Boca

Babes are in a constant state of starvation. Being on coke makes that easier.

After the server left she said, "Sweetie, I also wanted to see you because, well, I'm just beside myself. I don't know what to do. I thought maybe, you know, as a widow yourself you might have some words of wisdom."

Well, the circumstances of our widowhood were hardly the same. And it was damn weird to have her asking me for advice. But I went along, just to see where she was going.

"I just don't know how you do it, being all alone," she said, her eyes filling with tears.

"It's not easy," I said. "It takes time to adjust. But then the feeling of self-sufficiency is a real high." Higher than your coke, I wanted to add.

"I don't think I can face it," she said, choking back sobs.

She pulled herself together when the server came with our food.

"Give yourself some time," I said. "Lapidus just

passed, so you need to grieve. And take time to figure out who you are without him."

"But that's impossible. I'm nobody without a man. You know that."

Gee, thanks for just calling me a nobody. If that's how she felt, what the hell was she doing here?

"I need to find someone new," she went on. "But, you know, it's a jungle out there. All the men in Boca are cheap, domineering liars."

"And you just now figured this out?" I asked.

"Well, yes. You see, some of our friends have been out there on the dating scene."

Her friends, I thought. Not mine.

"Do you remember Randi?" she asked.

"Yeah." Like Gitta, Randi had married a much older man.

"Well, you know, she figured she was safe with Rupert. I mean, even though he'd been married four times before, she always thought she'd be his last wife. He was thirty-five years older, so she thought the chances of him leaving her for another woman were pretty slim. But guess what, that's exactly what happened. Right after she turned forty he left her for a twenty-three-year-old. And he's seventy-five!"

"Uh-huh," I said. This news did not come as a shock to me. I've been in Boca a long time.

"So she goes out to the clubs to meet somebody, right? She's aiming younger this time. So she meets a guy that seems very nice. They make a date for dinner. She gets all dressed up, with the high heels and push-up bra and everything. So then he comes over—with a pizza box!"

"Uh-huh."

"He puts the pizza in the kitchen, goes and sits on the couch, turns on the TV, and asks her to bring him a couple slices and a beer. So she does, and brings a couple for herself. Then when she gets up to get a third slice, he tells her she doesn't need to eat more than two. So then she puts the remaining slices in a container and puts them in the refrigerator and throws away the box. And do you know what he does then?"

"Uh-huh."

"You do?"

"Yeah. He tells her he wanted to take the rest home."

"How did you know that?"

I shrugged.

"So that was Mr. Cheap," she said. "Now, do you remember Tiffani?"

I stared at her. "Yes," I snapped.

"Oh, yes, of course you do. I'm sorry," Gitta said, flustered.

Tiffani was the woman at whose wedding reception I'd deep-sixed Bruce. That had brought the festivities to, well, an abrupt finale. Needless to say, Tiffani hadn't spoken to me since.

Gitta looked around the room and then whispered, "Scott was convicted of tax evasion and is in prison."

"Uh-huh." Again, no big shock there.

"So Tiffani divorced him. Then she went to one of those speed-dating things to meet somebody. So, you're in a room with like, twenty guys, and you get a minute to talk to each one, then you mark down if you like them and they mark if they like you. If there's a match the coordinator gives you each other's phone numbers."

"Uh-huh."

"So she gets a match and this guy calls her. Now, first of all, she can't even remember which one he is. I mean, when you've met twenty guys in twenty minutes, how can you remember, right?"

"Right."

"Well, they agree to meet for dinner and when she gets to the restaurant she does remember him, and remembers that she really liked him. So he treats her to a really nice dinner at La Paloma. He's a real gentleman throughout and he pays for dinner so she's getting really excited about him."

"Yeah."

"Then he suggests they go to her place to watch a DVD. She says fine. I mean, of course she understands what he's really talking about, and it's okay with her because she really likes this guy. They get to her house, she pours some wine and they pick out a DVD. But somehow they can't get it to run. So do you know what happens?"

"Uh-huh."

"You do?"

"Yeah. He yells at her for not knowing how to operate her DVD player, for not reading the owner's manual from cover to cover, and then not being able to find it."

"How did you know that?"

Again, I shrugged.

She took a bite of salad. "So that was Mr. Domineering. And do you remember Traci?"

"Yeah," I said wearily. I was getting pretty tired of her little gossip game. But I hadn't finished my sandwich yet, so I let her go on.

"Well, Brett died of a coke overdose a few months ago," she said.

I gave her what I thought was a meaningful look, but she was oblivious, being totally wrapped up in herself.

"So Traci went on one of those Internet dating sites," she continued, rambling. "She finds a really good-looking guy and he likes her looks, too, so they agree to meet. When she meets him for cappuccino, do you know what happens?"

Here we went again. "Uh-huh." This time I didn't wait for her response. "He's twenty years older, fifty pounds heavier and a hundred-percent balder than his picture on the Web site."

Again I didn't wait for her astonished response. I cut right to the shrug.

"So that was Mr. Liar," I said, preempting her yet again.

"Yes. But do you know the worst part of all this?" she asked.

"Uh-huh. Those women are still dating those guys."

This time she didn't even bother to ask how I knew.

"Right!" she said. "So that's the thing, sweetie. I just can't face the dating scene. Except I'm terrified of being alone." She started sobbing again. "All these years, I've kind of, well, admired you for your independence. That's why I wanted to talk to you."

She admired me? Wow, that was weird. I was just living my life to suit me. I didn't give a rat's ass about impressing anybody.

"Well, Gitta, like I said, take some time. Enjoy your children. Don't rush into anything."

She took a deep breath.

"Okay. I think you're right. I can do it. I can." She took another deep breath.

"And you might want to think about getting some help with your, uh, use."

"Oh, sweetie, that's nothing. You know I only use a little. Just to get a little lift, to keep me going through the day."

Right. Mother's little helper.

"You know how tiring life in Boca can be," she said.

Yeah, spending all day shopping, gossiping and beautifying sure could be exhausting.

Gitta may once have been the reigning queen of Boca, but now she was the queen of denial. But, hell, it wasn't my place to save her from herself. Was it? Besides, I'd finished my lunch and she didn't look too interested in the salad.

"Listen, Gitta," I said. "I've got an appointment to go to. It was nice to see you. I hope you'll think about what I said."

"Sure, I will, sweetie. Thank you. Will you call me sometime? I still have the same number."

"I don't remember it."

"Oh." She wrote it down on a napkin and handed it to me.

"Okay. Goodbye. Take care," I said.

I laid down money for my share of the bill and walked out, leaving her gazing out the window.

Damned if I didn't almost feel sorry for her.

I walked back to my office for my bike and rode over to Dennis Pearlman's office for our appointment. As I rode, I thought about Gitta. I still didn't think she was involved in the attempt on my life. She seemed to be in genuine pain and searching for solace. But why did she have to pick me? I had enough problems of my own, what with solving a murder and dealing with…relationships. Okay, yes, *a* relationship. I revved up the throttle to drive that thought out of my mind.

PEARLMAN'S VITAMIN COMPANY was located in a grimy industrial area off I-95 in Pompano Beach, a city south of Boca. Were it not for the security cameras all over the property, you'd never suspect that hundreds of millions in revenues were generated there annually. I was escorted to his office, whose plush interior was incongruous with the rest of the building.

He rose from behind his desk. He was sixtyish, pudgy and pale, with brittle hair and nails. Sure as hell not a walking advertisement for his own products.

"Please sit, Ms. Horowitz," he invited. "What can I do for you?"

"Well, sir, I'm a private investigator. I've been hired to look into the murder of the Reverend Botay, to whose church you recently made a sizable contribution."

"Wait a minute. My girl said you were with the media."

"Oh, dear, did she? There must have been a misunderstanding. I'm so sorry. I know how valuable your time is, so if you'd rather reschedule…"

"No, no, that's all right," he said irritably. "As

long as you're here, let's go ahead. So you're investigating this murder. I thought the killer was already identified."

I briefly explained that my unnamed clients thought the real killer was still at large.

"I see. Well, I'm deeply dismayed by the reverend's tragic death. So I'm eager to help you in whatever way I can, although, honestly, I don't see how."

"Can you tell me your reason for your donation to her church?"

"Well, as you surely know, I make numerous donations to worthy causes. This community has given me a great deal. My business is flourishing, so I'm more than happy to give back."

"Uh-huh."

"Besides, it's tax time and my accountant suggested that a write-off would be prudent," he said with a sheepish smile. "So there you have it. My motives may not be entirely altruistic, but they're certainly not murderous. I had no reason to kill that poor woman."

"I'm not suggesting that you did. I'm merely

gathering all kinds of information to look for possible connections."

"I see."

"How did you decide on the Church of the Gender-Free God for your donation?"

"Oh, I have an advisory board that makes recommendations to me. I like to diversify my giving. So my board looks at various programs, assesses their effectiveness, staffing, fiscal accountability and so forth. Then I select from among those they recommend. My selections are based on gut feeling. That's how I've always run my business. Get the facts first, then go with your instincts. Works every time."

"Okay, you've been very helpful," I said. "Thanks for your time."

"If you find some connection, let me know, will you?"

"By all means." I rose to leave.

"By the way, you do take your daily vitamins, don't you?" he asked.

"Uh, no."

"Oh, young lady, you must take care of your health. Here, please take some samples."

He reached into his desk and shoved a bunch of foil-encased pills into my hand.

"Now believe me, once you try these, you'll find energy and vitality that you never knew you had. Not to mention an unbelievable increase in libido."

He looked me up and down.

"I see you might be reaching an age where that may be a looming issue."

I dug my nails into the palms of my hands to keep from slugging him.

"And bear in mind," he went on, "we have a special offer for a lifetime supply."

"Yeah, thanks," I cut him off and rushed out the door. I tossed the pills in a Dumpster on my way to the bike.

I mounted the hog and turned on the ignition. The feel of that powerhouse vibrating between my legs reassured me that I had no lack of libido, thank you very much.

I rode back to the office, reflecting, as usual, on

the information I'd gained. It seemed pretty straight-forward. No obvious clues pointing to the killer.

At the office, I called Laurence Williams to update him on my activities and next steps.

"So you plan to infiltrate a white supremacist group in the middle of the night in the middle of nowhere? I'm not sure I like that idea."

"Hey, did you hire me for this case or not? If you don't like my methods, you're free to hire another…"

"Oh, come on, don't get your panties in a bunch."

I didn't bother informing him that thongs don't bunch up, since they're already riding up there. As a drag queen, he surely knew that, anyway.

"Just be careful, Harriet. Don't do anything reckless."

"Sure."

Reckless—who, me?

CHAPTER 12

That night I rode out on Hooker Highway to the assigned spot of Morse's gathering. The day's heat had cooled, the stars shone brightly and the sugarcane swayed in the breeze along both sides of the road. A gorgeous setting for such an ugly conclave.

I arrived at the old sugar mill, a long-deserted structure of rusted steel and scattered machinery that loomed over the flat landscape. Several pickup trucks were parked off the dirt road that led to the mill. I stopped to look them over. They weren't in top shape, with rusted fenders, balding tires and numerous dents. It was safe to say that the Loyal Brotherhood of Assholes did not hail from Boca, but from less fortunate parts of the county. They were probably struggling economically and feeling displaced from society, so they took the easy way out—scapegoating minorities, blaming them for the Brotherhood's plight, instead of getting off their own asses and doing something to better their lives.

In addition to the wear and tear, I noticed that a couple of the trucks had bullet holes in them. Well, road rage is a way of life in South Florida, so I wasn't surprised. Upon closer inspection, though, I saw that the bullet holes weren't real. They were fake. Stickers made to look like a bullet had penetrated the metal. Unbelievable. Jeez, maybe these guys were from Boca after all. I mean, everything is artificial in Boca, so why not bullet holes? Was this some new kind of status symbol? A way for disaffected youth to claim an identity? "I've been shot at, therefore I am?" But if that was the case, why fake it? Why not just get your gun and shoot up your own truck?

I had my Magnum stashed in my boot so I could oblige these guys if they desired…or pissed me off.

I rode on and saw the light of a fire up ahead. As I approached I saw a group of seven white men in their teens and early twenties sitting around a campfire, the flames alternately casting their faces in light and shadow. The men all wore red robes and fezzes, and were drinking beer out of aluminum cans and smoking. They turned to the rumble of my hog. A skinny, pimply faced guy rose and came over to me as I pulled up and turned off the ignition.

"I'm Lucas Morse," he said when I removed my helmet. "You must be the TV chick. Didn't expect to see a woman on no hog. Nice bike. Your husband's?"

I wasn't there to challenge his sexist assumptions, so I played along. "Yeah, that's right. He lets me borrow it once in a while, and I'm really grateful. Of course, I'll reward him for his generosity tonight."

"Now, you're my kind of woman. Know how to please your man. If you ever decide to ditch your old man, give me a call."

"Sure. I'll do that. Now how about we got on with the meeting?"

I pulled my mini videocam out of my saddlebag.

"Okay, I'm ready to roll," I said. "Now I want you guys to really dramatize this. Television is getting more and more extreme. So you've got to make it really over-the-top to make an impression on my executive producer."

I was hoping that by hamming it up they'd get carried away and let something slip if they'd had anything to do with the reverend's murder.

"Gotcha," Morse said. "Okay, brothers, let's gather around the fire."

I stepped back and turned on the camera.

They began chanting in unison, "We, the Loyal Brotherhood of Aryans, pledge to preserve these United States of America as the white Christian nation of our founding fathers. We gather around this fire, which represents the light of Christ. We unite to promote the gospel of racial separation and to fight the plot to destroy Western civilization. We condemn…"

Now they went around the circle, each one denouncing a particular group.

"Race-mixing."

"Homos and dykes."

"Hairy-legged women's libbers."

"Christ-killing Jews."

"Negroes."

"Immigrants."

"Pope-worshipping Catholics."

Well, that just about covered everyone I knew and loved.

"All hail to white Christian supremacy for the restoration of moral values in these great United States," they concluded in unison, raising their arms *Sieg Heil* style.

It was all I could do to keep myself from pulling my Magnum out of my boot and showing them who really held supremacy here.

"That's great, guys," I choked out. "My boss is going to love this. I can almost guarantee you'll be signed for *American Patriot*. But he might want more detail. So tell me about some of the actions you've taken to further your cause."

"We're very politically active," Morse said. "We hold rallies, speak to church youth groups, circulate petitions and we're planning a run for public office."

Hmm, which public office would that be? Village idiot?

Still, they'd said nothing about painting swastikas or killing uppity black women ministers.

As if reading my mind, Morse went on.

"A lot of folk got the wrong ideas about us. We ain't no hate group. We don't hate nobody. We just think these United States belong to the white man, and those other groups can find their own places on earth somewhere else. A lot of folk think we're violent, like we do lynchings and stuff. No way. Like I said, we are simply promoting a political agenda, as is our right as citizens of this great land."

"So you're very misunderstood," I said.

He failed to grasp the sarcasm in my voice.

"Yeah, exactly! *You* get it, why can't everybody else? You're pretty smart for a woman. You'll make sure we get on the show, right?"

"Sure, I'll be in touch," I said. "Don't call us, we'll call you."

As I was putting the camera away, a white Cadillac pulled up. Pastor Fred Hollings climbed out of the driver's seat. Okay, now the situation became clearer. Hollings was the hidden puppet master behind this bunch of whack-jobs.

He took a look at me.

Shit. My cover was blown and a blowup was about to ensue.

"What's *she* doing here?" he demanded.

"She's a TV producer," Morse said. "We're gonna be on one of them reality shows."

"No, you idiots," Hollings yelled. "She's a private eye. She's got you bamboozled."

"What?" they yelled and came at me.

As Morse bore down on me, I kicked him in the chest and he went down. Another one approached and I kneed him in the groin.

I had three down and four to go when I heard a distant rumble. It was the familiar rhythm of hogs in harmony. Then they rolled around the corner— the Holy Rollers, in drag, no less.

They dismounted, and the real battle began. Hollings locked himself in his Caddie as robes, fezzes, sequined dresses, wigs, girdles and bras went flying.

CHAPTER 13

I was the only one whose clothes remained intact. I guess there's something to be said for clean, simple, formfitting lines.

The Rollers and I kicked the Aryans' white butts and rode off in victory with a thunderous roar. As soon as we reached the edge of town, I pulled off the road and took off my helmet. The Rollers pulled up beside me. With their wigs gone, their dresses and undergarments in tatters, but their makeup intact, they presented a bizarre blend of male and female elements.

"What's up?" Lady Fingers asked.

I lost it.

"What the hell did you guys, uh, ladies, think you were doing?"

"Sweetie, we were worried about you," Virginia Hamm said. "We had an engagement this evening but afterward we had this bad feeling that you were in trouble so we felt that we had to come to your rescue."

"My what? My rescue? Do I look like a damsel in distress to you? Where do you guys get off with this sexist attitude? And you being drag queens, no less. Don't you find that just a little bit ironic? You hired me to do an investigation. So get the hell out of my way and let me do it!"

They hung their heads.

"We're sorry," Cherise Jubilee said. "We'll let you run the show from now on."

"Oh, hell." I sighed. "I'm the one that should be sorry. I want to do it all myself. That's why I snapped at you. I'm sorry and I'm grateful for your help."

"We don't want Wonder Woman," Keisha LaReigne said. "We want Dirty Harriet. All you have to be is you."

Now I hung my head. They'd just given me the gift of pure acceptance. How rare was that?

"Thanks," I mumbled.

Then I fired the hog back up, put on my helmet and headed for home.

I SPENT THE NEXT MORNING, Friday, recuperating from the battle. I took a long hot shower (well, as long as my small water tank would allow), then sat down in my rocking chair on the porch to bask in the sun. Lana was nowhere in sight. Since it was springtime, she was probably off somewhere mating. It was a pretty sad state of affairs if a gator was getting more action than I was.

Just as that thought passed through my mind, the phone rang.

"Horowitz, where are you?" It was Lior. "Why aren't you in class?"

"Huh?" I said.

"Your twelve o'clock class."

"Oh. I had a rough night. But believe me, I got enough Krav Maga practice to make up for a couple classes."

"What happened?" he asked, and I explained.

"So you're beat up and all alone."

"Yep, that's about the sum of it."

"Well, I'm coming out to bring you some matzo-ball soup and give you a massage."

"What? No way. I don't need anything. I'm fine."

"Sure. See you in a few hours."

What the hell was wrong with him? Had he just turned into a Jewish mother?

I didn't need any man to take care of me, for Christ's sake. Hadn't I worked long enough to become the independent superchick that I was? Why did he have to come along and disrupt my well-ordered existence?

But come along he did as promised—or threatened. He pulled up in a canoe, tied it to the porch and disembarked, bearing a plastic container.

This was weird. I'd never had company here in my remote hideaway.

His size seemed to overwhelm the small porch. He wore black jeans and a white T-shirt that stretched over his pecs and biceps.

His dark eyes looked me up and down, noting

the bruises and scratches on my bare arms. "You look like shit," he said.

"Thank you, that's very kind of you. How'd you find this place, anyway?"

"Horowitz, do you forget that I'm a former high-ranking officer of the Israeli defense? Do we ever have trouble finding who we're after? Besides, this was child's play. I just used my GPS tracker to get your coordinates from your cell phone."

Great. I guess I could run from civilization, but I couldn't hide.

"You got any eating utensils in this shack?" he asked.

"Yeah, they're in the kitchen. There are only two rooms, so I'm sure you can find it, ace tracker that you are."

He went in, then came out a few minutes later with a bowl of steaming soup and a spoon.

"I heated it on the stove," he said.

"Thanks," I grumbled and sipped a spoonful. Hmmm. It was piquant and buttery, with thick chunks of chicken and vegetables. This wasn't like any matzo-ball soup I'd ever had. Mine always came out of a can.

"Who cooked this?" I asked suspiciously. "Some girlfriend of yours?"

"Do I detect a hint of jealousy? Well, let me allay your fears. This is of my own making."

"You mean you cook?"

"I fail to see why you find it necessary to insult me. I do not cook, I create culinary sensations."

"No kidding."

Gee, it might be nice to have a hot-looking chef around to serve—and service—me. Why, it would be like having a wife.

There I went again. I didn't need this complication in my life. I was doing just fine as a loner.

I finished the soup while he sat in silence beside me on the wooden floorboards of the porch.

"Well, thanks a lot," I said. "I feel better now. You can go."

"Hold on, that was only part one of your therapy. Part two is the massage."

"That's really not necessary."

But he'd already gotten up, set the bowl aside and stood behind me with his hands on my shoulders. Before I knew it, a long "Ohhh" escaped my lips. I leaned back in my rocking chair until my head rested against him and closed my eyes as he continued to gently knead my aching shoulders and neck. I was drifting off to sleep when I felt his lips atop my head. Then those lips traveled softly and slowly to my ear, then my neck. His hands slid around me and cupped my breasts. I moaned.

Suddenly a huge splash of dirty swamp water hit us both square in the face. Lior pulled back and I wiped the scum from my eyes. When I opened them I saw Lana whipping her tail and sporting a shit-eating grin.

My faithful neighbor had come to my rescue just as I was about to slide down the slippery slope of sexual surrender.

I leaped out of my rocking chair. It rocked back and hit Lior right in the anatomical part under consideration.

"Shit," he cried and collapsed to the ground.

"Jesus," I said, kneeling beside him. "Are you all right?"

"Yeah, I'll be fine," he croaked.

"Can I do anything?"

"No, I think your diabolical pet has done enough."

So I just sat beside him for ten minutes, my hand on his arm, until he finally sat up.

"I'm sorry," I said.

"You are? Well, in that case, you can make up for it. Come with me to Shabbos services tonight and ask for forgiveness." Shabbos, the Jewish day of rest, started at sundown on Fridays.

"What? Are you nuts?"

"Actually, yeah, right now all I feel is nuts."

."Look, you know I'm not religious. And I'm only half-Jewish, on my father's side."

"So expand your horizons a little. You owe me."

"Fine. Fine. Let's go." I didn't even know why I said that. Did I really believe I owed him something? Did I just want to get him off my back? Or did I actually care for him? No, that couldn't be it. Uh-uh.

"Fine."

"I'll have to change at the office, though."

"At the office?"

"Yeah, that's where I stash my one suit. It's normally for undercover operations. But I can't go to temple like this." I gestured to my black stretch leggings and tank top.

"Right. I'll follow you to your office."

We tied his canoe to my airboat and took off for land. Once there, he fastened the canoe onto a rack on top of his Jeep. I rolled my hog off the airboat, climbed on and we rode separately to my office.

He waited in the Jeep while I went in and changed into the suit, a white Dolce & Gabbana with a short skirt and fitted jacket and matching four-inch vamp shoes. It was the one outfit I'd kept from my Boca Babe days. Then I reached deep into my bottom desk drawer and pulled out my secret stash, a Ziploc bag stuffed with leftovers. Not food—cosmetics. Again from my past life. I went into the bathroom and applied the stuff.

Finally I emerged from the office, locked the door and climbed into Lior's Jeep. He gave me a long, slow stare from the top of my head to my tit cleavage to my toe cleavage.

"Who are you?" he asked. "What did you do with Horowitz? Have you got her tied up in there?"

"Very funny," I said. "Let's just go."

Ten minutes later we arrived at the Temple Beth Boca, a large, white modernist structure with an irregular gabled roof that rose to a triangular peak with Chagall stained glass on two sides. As we pulled up, I had a sickening sense of déjà vu from Chuck and Enrique's wedding. But wait. This wasn't a déjà vu. It really was a repeat performance. Police cars were everywhere, red lights flashing. The white CSI van was there again, as was the throng of celebrity-seekers.

A few well-dressed men and women, apparently congregants, were gathered in a corner of the lawn under a royal palm tree. We got out of the Jeep and walked over to them. I stumbled as my fricking four-inch heels sank into the soft ground. Lior took my hand. I wanted to pull away, but I wanted more to find out what was going on. So I let him hold on until we reached the group.

"What's happening?" Lior asked.

A matronly woman with a head of platinum helmet hair came up to him and grabbed him.

"Lior, darling, you haven't heard? The rabbi…" she sobbed. "The rabbi has been killed."

"What? How? When?"

"Strangled with his own prayer shawl. This morning, they say."

Lior's face turned pale.

"But I just saw him here this morning. He was fine when I left. I can't believe it."

At that moment Detective Reilly came up to the group. He took a quick look at me, eyes narrowed.

"Detective Horowitz? Is that you? At another of my crime scenes?"

Before I had a chance to reply, he turned to Lior.

"Lior Ben Yehuda, you are under arrest for the murder of Rabbi Lev Zelnik."

CHAPTER 14

The congregants and I looked on helplessly as two uniformed cops handcuffed Lior and hauled him off. Infuriated, I stalked after Reilly, who was conferring with the crime-scene investigators.

"What the hell's going on?" I demanded. "Why'd you arrest Lior?"

Reilly slowly turned to me.

"Ms. Horowitz," he said evenly, "I would like to have a chat with you. Shall we go inside for a cup of coffee?"

More déjà vu. I followed him into the temple and down a hallway into a kitchen. A pot of coffee was already brewed, and he poured me a cup.

"I know, black, no sugar," he said as he handed

it to me. He poured one for himself and said, "Let's go sit."

He led me into the main part of the temple and we sat in a pew. The setting sun filtered through the stained-glass tower above, casting multicolored hues around the room. Reilly was bathed in a pool of green. It did not enhance his pale, freckly Irish complexion. He looked like a frog with chicken pox. Red was shining on me. In that femme fatale Babe outfit, I probably looked like a scarlet harlot.

Reilly didn't seem to notice, though.

"Now, will you kindly explain what you're doing here?" he asked. "Do you habitually hang around religious murder sites?"

By now I'd calmed down a little. I figured I'd get more from him if we exchanged some tit-for-tat, so I ignored his snide remark and explained my presence.

"How long have you known Mr. Ben Yehuda?" he asked.

"A few years."

"And what is the nature of your relationship?"

Shit. How could I explain the nature of my relationship with Lior? I couldn't even explain it to myself.

"He's my Krav Maga instructor. Recently we've become…friendly."

"I see. Do you happen to know where he was this morning?"

"He said he was here."

"Were you with him?"

"No."

"Then how do you know he was here?"

"I didn't say I knew he was here, I said he said he was here."

"So you don't actually know if he was here."

"That's what I just said."

"You said he said he was here. You didn't say you didn't know if he was here."

"Exactly. That's what I said."

"Exactly what?"

Oh, my God. This had to stop.

"Look, let me be perfectly clear," I said slowly. "I do not know where Lior was this morning."

"Okay, that's all I was asking."

Jeez. "So now that you have my information, how about sharing a little of yours?" I asked.

"Well, seeing as you're a fellow investigator, albeit of a different sort," he said condescendingly, "I'll extend you the professional courtesy of giving you advance information that will shortly be released to the media, anyway."

"Gee, thanks."

"In fact, Mr. Ben Yehuda was here this morning, meeting with the rabbi."

"If you already knew that, why'd you ask me?"

"Please, Ms. Horowitz. You have your investigative methods, we have ours."

He took a sip of coffee, then continued, "Upon interviewing several members of the congregation, I learned that Mr. Ben Yehuda is the president of the synagogue, and that there has been some major discord among the temple members, which was the subject of his meeting with the rabbi."

"What kind of discord?"

"Apparently, it concerned the price of tickets for the High Holidays. The rabbi and some members felt that the tickets should have varied price levels, with the best seats costing the most. Like at a concert, right?"

"Yeah."

"Others, including Mr. Ben Yehuda, thought that the temple was no place for ostentatious displays of wealth. They argued that all tickets should be priced the same, with seats going on a first-come, first-served basis."

I stared at the man. "So you're suggesting that Lior killed the rabbi over some petty dispute over ticket prices?"

Reilly smiled indulgently. "Ms. Horowitz, you are clearly not a regular temple-goer or churchgoer. If you were, you would know that houses of worship are the scenes of some of the worst backbiting and backstabbing that you could ever imagine. Believe me when I say that these battles get way uglier than any catfights or dirty politics you may ever have witnessed. So yes, to answer your question, that is precisely what we think happened. And we have probable cause to arrest him."

"This is insane," I said. "There's no way Lior would…"

"Ms. Horowitz, you just said yourself that your relationship with this man has been quite superficial until recently. So you don't really know him all that well, do you?"

I swallowed hard. Could he be right? Could Lana have been right? Could I be involved with a killer?

I shoved that thought out of my mind.

"No way," I said. "That's just ridiculous. Don't you see there must be a connection between this murder and that of the Reverend Botay? Come on, what are the odds of two clergy in Boca being killed within days of each other?"

"There are no signs of a serial killer or a copycat killer. The methods of murder are totally different, as are the victims."

"But it doesn't have to be a serial or copycat killer, someone who kills just for thrills. It's the motive that could be the same. Don't these look like hate crimes to you? The Church of the Gender-Free God was pro-gay, and the temple is, obviously,

Jewish. And isn't this the temple that had swastikas painted on it a while back?"

"Yes. Nonetheless, we do not see these murders as connected."

"Well, I do. In fact, I have some suspects you should check out." I was thinking, of course, of Hollings, Morse and the Loyal Brotherhood of Assholes.

"Ms. Horowitz, we've already arrested and charged our suspects. Now if you have a different theory, you're certainly free to pursue it. But our job is done."

"Wow, your arm must really hurt, Reilly," I said.

"From what?"

"From patting yourself on the back."

I got up, turned on my heel and strode out. His job might be done, but mine sure as hell wasn't. I knew damn well that someone was out to send Boca's clergy to their heavenly rewards. And I would prove it.

CHAPTER 15

Sundown had come and Shabbos had arrived by the time I left the temple. But there would be no rest for me until this case was solved.

As I rode home, a light drizzle started to fall. I gently downshifted and slowed. Rain is a serious issue when a bike is your only form of ground transportation. A light sprinkling like this is okay if you take it nice and easy and don't need to look presentable wherever it is you're going. But a real downpour, the kind we get in South Florida every summer afternoon, will stop you in your tracks. Unless you're suicidal, you'll hide under the nearest overpass and wait it out.

When all you've got is your hog, you've got to be flexible. You've got to surrender to nature instead of riding roughshod over it with your self-imposed deadlines and pressures. That's why a lot of real bikers—not the weekend road warriors—operate outside the rat race. It's where we want to be.

As I rode through the mist, my mind entered that altered state induced by the sound of the pistons' syncopated repetitions. In this alternate frame of mind, I realized what my next step had to be. I had to find out what the two victims had in common that would have led to a single motive in their killings. The murders could be hate crimes, as I'd indicated to Reilly, but I still thought I needed to stay open to all possibilities. After all, my investigations of Hollings and Morse hadn't yielded anything solid about the Reverend Botay's murder.

By the time I got home, the drizzle had developed into a real shower. Inside the cabin, the noise of the heavy raindrops hitting the roof was intense. I dried myself off, got my Hennessy and went out to sit on the covered porch to observe nature's power.

My front "yard" contains a few mangrove trees,

distinctive for their gnarled, tangled, aboveground root systems. Now, their branches were bent over, hunched against the liquid onslaught. The fresh raindrops appeared to bounce off the murky swamp water before melding into it. A blue heron swooped onto the edge of the porch, stood tall, folded its six-foot wingspan into its sides and shook off the water. Nearby, tree frogs serenaded us with their croaks.

I love a good storm. I lost myself in its sounds, sights and smells.

Then Lana floated by, bringing me back to the day's events.

"How dare you show your snout after what you did today," I told her.

"Oh, get over it," she replied. "How many times have you said you don't want any romantic entanglements? I was only helping you."

Okay, maybe she actually had done me a favor. Especially if Lior really was a killer.

The thought made me sick. I couldn't deal with that possibility right now. Hey, even the justice system considered him innocent until proven guilty, so the least I could do was the same. And if he was proven guilty…well, I'd deal with that later.

I gave Lana the rundown on what had transpired that evening.

"So what do you think these two victims had in common, other than both being members of oppressed minority groups?" I asked her.

She stayed still, seemingly thinking it over.

Finally she said, "Well, you know that clergy members often serve together on various committees. Ecumenical councils, interfaith task forces, that kind of thing. So I'd look into that."

Just then, a bolt of lightning lit up the night sky, followed by a clap of thunder that shook the little cabin. Apparently, nature was backing Lana's suggestion big-time.

THE NEXT MORNING, THE RAIN had stopped. Leaves glistened in the sunlight, and the scent of renewal permeated the air.

I made coffee and called Lupe.

"Did you know that Rabbi Zelnik of Temple

Beth Boca was killed yesterday?" I dove right in, dispensing with pleasantries.

"Yes, I'm just sitting here reading about it in the paper. And they arrested Lior Ben Yehuda? Isn't that the guy you—"

"Yes, yes," I interrupted. I didn't want to get into another discussion about that relationship.

"Look, I think these murders are connected," I said.

"I'm inclined to agree with you."

"So I'm searching for similarities between the victims. Do you happen to know what community committees the Reverend Botay was on? If the rabbi was on one or more of the same ones, that could give us a lead to a motive."

"Yes, let's see... She was on the Coalition of Christians and Jews...the Islamic Support Network...the Domestic Violence Task Force... and the Citizens' Ethics Advisory Committee of the city council. There might have been others, but I can't think of any more right now."

"That's great, I'll start with those."

"They probably all have Web sites that list their membership and activities."

"Yeah, I bet you're right." Who didn't have a Web site these days? Except for me. ScamBusters was all about privacy, not publicity.

"Okay, thanks a lot, Lupe. I'll keep you posted." I hung up.

I PILOTED MY AIRBOAT THROUGH the gently swaying saw grass to land. Then I rode my hog to town. With the roads dry, I was able to open up the throttle and fly.

At the office, I logged on to the Internet. I Googled the committees Lupe had named, and their Web sites readily came up. I found that both the reverend and the rabbi served on the Coalition of Christians and Jews and the Islamic Support Network. Several other clergy were on those, as well, although not Pastor Hollings. Figured. His particular brand of religion was hardly inclusive of others. Neither the rabbi nor Hollings were on the Domestic Violence Task Force.

I went to the city council Web site and clicked on the Citizens' Ethics Advisory Committee. Both the reverend and the rabbi were on it, as was Hollings and another clergyperson, Father Murphy of Our Lady of the Fairways. There were also three laypeople: a bioethicist, a philosophy professor and, of all people, Dennis Pearlman, the vitamin magnate. How the hell did he get on there? Did he muscle his way in on account of his charitable contributions to the community? Or did he buy his way in? Could there be corruption in the city council? Perish the thought!

I scrolled down farther to look at what ethical issues were currently before the committee. I already knew that the same-sex marriage ordinance was one. Although that was a possible motive for the reverend's killing, I had no idea where the rabbi stood on the issue.

Apart from that, there were two other ethical issues before the committee. One concerned a proposal to ban the wearing of furs on public property. That included all city streets, effectively meaning that the beavers would be booted and the rabbits run out of town. Mink would be maligned and sable would be stigmatized.

Now, I know some Northerners might think, *What? People wear fur in Florida?*

Yep. Remember, this is Boca, land of Boca Babes and BOTOX Babes. When the temperature drops to sixty, the furs come out in droves. The streets look like a herd of buffalo is passing through.

Okay, I knew that some animal-rights activists had staged some ugly attacks against fur wearers up north, but was this really the kind of thing people would kill over? Well, maybe in Boca. The Babes could care less about stripping the animals of their coats, but when it came to stripping *them* of *theirs*… I might have to check it out, but I put it on the back burner for now.

The remaining ethical issue concerned a company called EternaLife, specialists in cryonics. They were seeking approval from the city council to open up shop in Boca to freeze dead folks, putting them in a state of suspended animation with the possibility of being thawed out and brought back to life at some point in the future, providing that became scientifically feasible. The company already owned a subsidiary in Boca—Preserve-A-Pet— which offered the service to Boca's bereaved who just couldn't bear to part with little Fido or Fifi. The firm now wanted to expand that service to humans.

Reading further, I saw that on the same day that I'd attended the council hearing on the same-sex marriage ordinance, they'd also held a hearing on EternaLife. Based on the minutes, the issue was highly contentious. There was testimony from company officials, scientific experts and the general public, weighing in on both sides.

Of course, the company's representatives and their experts lauded the venture as a major scientific advancement that would position Boca as a technological epicenter and stimulate an influx of other biotech companies, creating hundreds of high-paying jobs. Naturally, a tax incentive and city funds were requested in exchange for this promise of prosperity. And, of course, there was the unstated but obvious threat that if Boca didn't comply, the company would take its business and high-paying jobs elsewhere.

On the other side were scientists who testified that the idea of suspended animation was a hoax. The public opined on both sides, but the majority was in favor. As with the marriage ordinance, the council was now seeking a recommendation from the Ethics Committee.

As a ScamBuster, I immediately saw the Eterna-Life scheme for what it was. As far as I was concerned, the company might as well take its business to Disney World, since their so-called technology belonged in fantasyland. But as with all scams, I could understand its appeal to the gullible. After all, Boca, with its beaches, year-round sunshine, palatial homes, golf courses, lakes and Babes, was a paradise. If you had the possibility of spending eternity here, why not? Why take your chances in the great beyond? I mean, who knew what kind of shopping malls they had over there?

I sat back in my chair and rubbed my neck. All this was giving me a major headache. This town might be paradise, but with its iguana bridge, fur fight and frozen dead pets, Boca was driving me bonkers.

CHAPTER 16

I needed to clear my mind of all the Boca bizarreness. And, of course, there was only one way to do that. Hog riding.

I decided to ride up to the county jail to see Lior. I knew he'd still be there since he'd been booked on Friday night and there wouldn't be a hearing until Monday. I also knew what the visiting hours were, since it was the same jail I'd been in after offing my husband. Not that I'd had many visitors. Only one, in fact. The contessa. For some reason, she had believed in me. But apart from her, I had suddenly had no friends. The ones I have now have come along in my post-Babe phase.

I locked up the office, got on my hog and headed up the turnpike to West Palm Beach. As I rode, I felt my heartbeat synchronize with the thump-thump-thump of the bike's engine. When I left the Boca city limits, I left my headache behind.

I was in control and uninhibited. I noted the envious glances cast at me by women passengers riding in cages—biker terminology for cars—that were driven by men. As Susan B. Anthony said over a hundred years ago, a woman on two wheels is the picture of free, untrammeled womanhood.

So by the time I arrived at the jail, my mind was indeed clearer. I knew I had to clear the air with Lior.

After passing through multiple security checks and three sets of locked steel doors, I was ushered into the meeting room with its glass partition and phones on either side. Shortly thereafter, Lior was brought in.

His characteristic bravado was gone, replaced with a look of resignation. Despite his bulk, he looked shrunken in his oversize, jail-issued orange jumpsuit.

We sat on the two sides of the window and picked up the phones.

"Hi," he said. "I didn't expect to see you."

"Look, I'm going to get you out of here. First of all, I'm going to call the contessa. I think there's a connection between the rabbi's murder and a case I'm working on, the Reverend Botay's murder. You've heard about it?"

"Yeah."

"Once I explain this to the contessa I'm sure she'll bail you out. That woman has a keen sense of justice and puts her money where her mouth is."

"Forget about it. I'm sure they'll deny me bail. Since I've only been in this country for a few years, they'll consider me a flight risk."

"Well…at least the contessa can hook you up with S. Lee Dailey. He's the top defense lawyer in the county, and he's working on the other case."

"Thanks. But I think I'm toast."

"Look, help me out here. Do you know anyone who may have had a motive to kill the rabbi?"

"Well, there was a lot of dissension within the congregation, but I can't imagine anyone who would take it that far."

"What about outside the congregation? Are you aware that the rabbi served on several community committees?"

"Sure. But again, it's hard to imagine anyone from those killing him."

"Do you happen to know where the rabbi stood on gay rights issues?"

"Gay rights? No, I don't know. He never brought it up, not to the congregation, nor to me, either."

I took a deep breath. "What about you?"

I had to know where he stood, too. Not just because of the murders, but because of our... our...okay, our relationship. If Lior was opposed to gays, and my best friends were gay, how could we ever be compatible?

"Me? Why?"

"Just answer the question, please."

"Okay. I'm a member of a religious minority. I know what it means to be persecuted. The Nazis persecuted gays as well as Jews. So as far as I'm concerned, we're brothers and sisters in arms."

I let out my breath, which I wasn't even aware

I'd been holding. If he was telling the truth, then there just might be a future for us.

What the hell was I thinking? I needed to delve into the deaths, not fantasize about a future that I wasn't even sure I wanted. I had to get back on track.

"Okay," I told Lior. "Don't lose hope. I will spring you, you can count on that."

He didn't reply. We didn't do that sappy thing you see in the movies, where the people hold their hands up to each other across the glass. We just hung up and left.

I RODE HOME FOR MY NIGHTLY conferral with Lana.

"So what did you find the victims had in common?" she demanded as soon as I sat down with my Hennessy.

"Quite a lot. Three committees. That just broadens the scope of the investigation, instead of narrowing it."

I filled her in.

"I would look into that Ethics Committee," she said. "Those issues they're considering are of significant interest to me. You know, we in the animal kingdom have to stick together. If they don't ban the furs, they'll keep on raising those poor creatures just for their hides. You can see what would happen next, can't you?"

"No."

"They'd come after me, trying to turn me into ten purses for your Boca Babe friends."

"Hey, they aren't my friends anymore. Never were, actually. Anyway, I wouldn't let that happen to you."

She gazed at me with what looked suspiciously like affection. If she could have batted her eyelashes, she would have, but, of course, she didn't have any.

"Aw, shucks," she said. "And if I should go before you, will you put me in suspended animation at Preserve-A-Pet?"

Now I stared at her. "Yeah, right, so you can come back to life again and keep on tormenting me? I don't think so."

"Fine, be that way," she said, and turned away with a flip of her tail, sending the swamp water right into my face again.

Jeez, we sounded just like an old married couple. Albeit a pretty happy one. Okay, maybe not all marriages were like the one I'd had.

Oh, hell, my mind sure had been wandering in the romance direction a lot lately. It was time to give it a rest. But before I did, I thought about Gitta and her problems with romance, or lack thereof. A part of me identified with her. That had been me once, unable to imagine life without a man. That was the mental prison that Boca Babes lived in. I'd managed to break out; maybe I could help her do the same. Plus, I knew that any kind of recovery had to include sharing your insights with others. Otherwise, relapse was imminent.

I went inside the cabin, found the napkin with her phone number that I'd put in a drawer, and called.

"Gitta, it's Harriet Horowitz," I said when she answered. "Just calling to see how you're doing."

"Oh, sweetie, that's so thoughtful of you," she said in her babyish voice. "Actually, I'm doing better. I've joined one of those exclusive match-making services."

I cringed.

"This isn't anything like the clubs, the speed dating, or the Internet," she went on. "This service selects only the highest quality people. And it's not cheap, so you know the men they select have money. Harriet, I think this is exactly what I need. I haven't been matched with anyone yet, but I feel better already since I signed up. It gives me hope."

Great. She'd asked for my advice, then hadn't taken a word of it. I was sure she hadn't done anything about the coke habit, either. In fact, her almost elated tone led me to suspect that she'd just snorted some.

"Well, I'm glad you're feeling better," I lied. At least this time I didn't have anything in my mouth to choke on.

"Thank you, sweetie. You're a doll. Call me again sometime, will you?"

"Yeah, sure. Bye."

I hung up the phone and looked at the napkin with her number on it. I had no intention of calling her again. She'd made her choices. She'd have to find her own way. Really, in the end, that was the only way.

I AWOKE STRUGGLING FOR BREATH, tangled in wet sheets. Oh, no. Not again. Another nightmare. Not the shooting this time. A replay of one of Bruce's assaults. This one I hadn't remembered in years. They came like this from time to time, fighting their way up from the depths of my subconscious where I'd shoved them and, I'd thought, locked them away.

As I lay there trying to even out my breathing, the fragments of the memory came together.

I'm in my old home, setting the table with sterling, crystal and candlelight for an intimate dinner with my husband. I've picked up an order of veal marsala from La Cucina Toscana, our favorite Italian gourmet market. I hear Bruce come in the door. I wait for the signs that will tell me what kind of mood he's in. Our shih tzu, Diva Dog, scampers to the door to greet him.

"Hi, poochie," I hear him say. "Come on, give Daddy a big kiss. Daddy had a great day. Where's Mommy? Let's go tell her all about it."

My shoulders relax, my jaw unclenches. He's in

a good mood tonight. Everything's okay. We'll have a nice evening.

I go to the foyer, where he's holding Diva as she licks his face. He sets her down and kisses me. I smell his breath for alcohol. None. I relax more and lengthen the kiss. He pulls me closer and slaps my ass playfully.

"Who's the hottest lawyer in town?" he asks.

"Oh, gosh, let me think about that," I say, playing along. "Old 'Barracuda' Bartholomew?"

"Nope. You're lookin' at him." He grins. "You know that woman who sued her obstetrician for letting her labor go on too long and depriving the baby of oxygen?"

"Yeah."

"Her lawyers finally caved. Said she can't take the stress of the lawsuit together with caring for this special-needs kid anymore. So they're accepting an out-of-court settlement for a pittance, with a gag order to boot. So am I hot or am I hot?"

I don't want to answer. I don't want to hear

about the morally questionable source of the income that fuels our lifestyle.

But he doesn't want an answer, anyway. He already has his own.

"How about a glass of champagne to celebrate?" he asks.

I hesitate, but don't want to ruin his mood. I know he can switch in the blink of an eye.

"Sure," I say.

We walk into the living room and he and Diva sit on the white leather couch while I go to the temperature-controlled wine room. I get a bottle of Cristal and take it to him along with two flute glasses. I sit down beside him as he pops the cork. He pours and we clink our glasses.

"By the way, honey, did you pick up my dry cleaning like I asked you to this morning?" he asks.

"Oh. No, sweetie, I didn't have time today, but I figured I'd go first thing in the morning. They open at seven so you'll have plenty of time to get dressed and get to work."

His eyes freeze and his face goes rigid.

"I told you to pick it up today."

"I know, but like I said…"

"I heard you. You didn't do what I asked. I work my ass off to provide you with this—" he sweeps his arm around to indicate the house, spilling champagne on himself "—and all I ask is for you to do one simple thing for me and you can't manage to do it."

I back away from him. "I don't see what the problem is. If I get the clothes at seven in the morning, you can still wear them tomorrow."

"She doesn't see what the problem is," he mocks my words to Diva, who has now jumped off the couch and is hiding behind it. "The problem is I asked you to do something and you didn't do it," he screams. "The problem is you're a sorry excuse for a wife. All you think about is yourself, you worthless piece of shit."

He grabs the champagne bottle and smashes it down on the glass-topped coffee table. The tabletop shatters into big jagged pieces.

I jump up and run to the far side of the room, to the dining table that I'd set.

"I'm leaving," I say. "I'll come back when you've calmed down."

"Get the hell out," he yells. Then he picks up one of the glass pieces and flings it at me. It flies through the air like a Frisbee. I put my hands up to protect my face. The jagged edge hits my forearm. Burning pain sears all the way up to my shoulder.

I grab a linen napkin off the dining-room table and press it to my arm to stop the blood flow. Then I grab my car keys and run out of the house.

But later that night I come back. And the next morning at seven I pick up his dry cleaning.

The piercing cry of a limpkin bird outside jarred me back to the present. I gazed out the window at the foot of my bed. The pale light of dawn was coming through. I lay still, thinking about the dream. I was starting to see a connection. Every time I thought about romance or marriage, these dreams would come. Okay, so all I had to do was avoid those subjects. Just as I had been doing for the last four years.

There was no way I'd get back to sleep now. Might as well get started on the day.

I got up and made coffee. After drinking it, I still felt shaky. I needed to regain my balance, and I knew just how to do that. Motorcycle maintenance. If you own a hog, maintenance is an integral part of the experience. If you won't keep it up, don't saddle up.

I pulled the bike off the airboat onto the porch and set it on its center stand. I cleaned, wiped and polished every surface. Then I went through the standard safety checks of tires, wheels, controls, lights, oil and chassis. By the time I was done, Doormat Harriet was gone and Dirty Harriet was back.

Just in time, too, because the phone rang, and when I picked it up, the voice at the other end said, "Harriet, the most horrible thing happened!"

CHAPTER 17

Who else but Mom, the drama queen? What was it now? Before I had a chance to ask what horrible thing had happened, she went on.

"Last night Howard Levine, Leonard and I attended a protest against the iguana statues. The protest was right on the bridge. It was so crowded, just jam packed, like the Ponte Vecchio…"

Oh, please. Was she seriously comparing a little concrete span over a canal with the world-renowned medieval Florentine landmark? What did I say—drama queen. I kept my mouth shut.

"Well, in all the melee, poor Howard was pushed off the bridge into the canal!"

"Is he all right?"

"Yes, now. But it was terribly frightening. Some

young men pulled him out and an ambulance took him to the hospital. Of course, we went there after him, but they wouldn't tell us anything except that he was stable. You know how tight-lipped they are, with those new privacy laws. But he called this morning and said he'd been released and was fine."

"Well, I'm sorry for your distress, Mom, but it seems to be okay now."

"No, it's not okay. First the reverend, then the rabbi and now Howard. For all we know, someone tried to kill Howard."

"Maybe, but it sounds like an accident to me. And it doesn't seem to fit the pattern of the killings. But how do you know about the rabbi, anyway?"

"As a matter of fact, Harriet, I had to hear about him from Howard himself last night. He's a member of the congregation. My own daughter was at the scene, her boyfriend was arrested and she couldn't be bothered to let her mother know."

"He's not my boyfriend!" was the first thing that came out of my mouth.

I took a deep breath. I wasn't going to get into it with her.

When she realized that, she went on. "Well, surely your boyfr—I mean, Lior, did not kill the rabbi."

"I'm looking into it, Mom."

"Maybe it was a domestic dispute. I heard the rabbi's wife was about to divorce him. Maybe she decided she'd be better off widowed than divorced. Like you."

So now I was a role model for wrathful wives?

"Uh-huh," I said. "So she killed the reverend, too?"

"No… Oh, I don't know. It's all so overwhelming. I'm just trying to help."

"I appreciate that, Mom. But I'm on top of it. I might follow up on the domestic angle, but I'm pursuing other leads right now."

"All right, dear. You may be right. Now about that dinner we talked about a few days ago? How's tomorrow night, six o'clock? And since you refuse to bring Lior, well actually, since he can't come, anyway, why don't I invite Chuck and Enrique? I think they said they'd be back today from their, uh, pseudohoneymoon, and I'm sure they'd appreciate a warm welcome home."

"Yeah. Sure. Fine. See you then."

Anything to get her off the phone.

Once I hung up, though, her words began to nag at me. What if this really was as simple as a domestic case? Could I be complicating matters with my conspiracy theory?

I decided it wouldn't hurt to check out the supposedly merry widow. I figured the family would be sitting shivah, the traditional Jewish seven-day formal mourning period, so I could drop in to pay my respects.

I loaded up the bike onto the airboat and sped off for land. Once there, I stopped by my office and looked up the rabbi's address in the phone book. The house was in one of Boca's innumerable country-club developments.

I rode over and announced myself to the ever-present gatehouse guard.

"Yes, ma'am," he said. "The family is receiving visitors all day today. Please go ahead."

He lifted the gate bar and I cruised through.

I easily found the house, as cars overflowed from its driveway onto the street. This was good. I could blend right in. Maybe I wouldn't even have to ask any questions. I knew from experience that you could learn a lot just by listening.

I rang the bell. A medium-height, droopy-eyed guy in his thirties answered the door. A yarmulke nestled in this curly brown hair.

I introduced myself. "I'm here to pay my respects," I said.

"Please come in. I'm Abe Zelnik, the rabbi's older son."

"I'm so sorry for your loss," I said.

"Thank you. I'm sure my mother will appreciate your coming by. She's over there."

He gestured across the room to a sixtyish woman sitting in a thronelike wicker chair underneath a mirror draped in black cloth. She wore a long black dress, had black hair and a long straight nose. Damned if she didn't look like an older version of Morticia Adams.

The room was full of black-clad, skullcapped mourners. A line of people waited to speak with the widow, who seemed to be holding court.

"Thanks," I told Abe and walked over to take my place in line.

As I waited, I eavesdropped on the conversation around me.

Two older women stood in front of me. Based on their similar features, I figured they were sisters. One of them was saying to the other, "Rachel, did you hear that the rabbi left $30,000 to be used for his funeral?"

"Really?" the other woman asked.

"Yes! And I hear there's absolutely nothing left!"

"How can that be, Leah?" Rachel asked.

"Well, I'm told the funeral cost was $6,500. And I heard Mrs. Z made a donation to the synagogue for $500 and she spent another $1,000 for food and drinks for this shivah. The rest went for the memorial stone."

"Twenty-two thousand dollars for the memorial stone?" Rachel asked. "My God, how big is it?"

"Four and a half carats," Leah replied.

Hmm, I thought. Maybe the widow really had done him in.

I tuned back into the conversation, hoping to pick up more info. Unfortunately, the women had shifted to another topic.

"What a shame you couldn't make it to Rex's bark mitzvah, Rachel," Leah was saying.

Had I heard that right? A *bark* mitzvah?

"It was the most fabulous party," Leah continued. "All the doggy guests got kosher treats and there was a beautiful cake from the dog bakery, and you should have seen the decorations! Our colors were black and gold, and all the guests got black patent-leather collars with real gold thread trim. I tell you, my party planner really outdid herself."

"That's nice, Leah," Rachel said, "but I doubt yours outdid the Blumensteins' bark mitzvah for their little Rex. The party was held in a hot air balloon."

God help us. I had heard right. A bark mitzvah. Apparently a coming-of-age ritual for your pampered pooch. Only in Boca. I wanted to ask what exactly they do at a bark mitzvah. Read from the Pet-ateuch? And what do Catholic canines have? Con-fur-mation? It was all dogma to me.

Leah went on, "Well, Rachel, of course the Blumensteins have no sense of decorum. That's exactly the kind of tacky showiness I'd expect from them."

"I beg to differ," Rachel said.

"Hmmph," Leah sniffed.

Rachel apparently decided to change the subject, yet again. "Did you hear that Rhoda passed?" she asked.

"Yes, I heard!" Leah replied. "I was shocked. It was so unexpected."

"Yes, you just never know," Rachel said.

Well, I reflected, that is just a reality of life in Boca. When you live in a retirement haven like this, a certain amount of death comes with the territory.

Then Rachel went on, "Yes, that cosmetology exam is really tough, but she passed."

"Well, good for her," Leah said. "You know, maybe she could be my new hairstylist. My Lorenzo is leaving the salon."

"He is? Why?"

"Imagine this. After all this time we've been together and I've poured out my heart and soul to him, he tells me he really doesn't like people. So he's going to open his own salon in one of those assisted-living facilities. He figures that's one population he can deal with. They're not really demanding. Plus, he'll have a steady supply of clientele right there, so he won't have to troll for patrons."

Again I wanted to jump right into the conversation, and ask why Lorenzo was setting his sights so low. I mean, if he really wanted a nondemanding, steady supply of clientele, why not go all the way— to the funeral homes? After all, this is Boca. Everybody wants to look good right up to the very end.

Mercifully, the women's discussion finally ended as they reached the front of the line and expressed their condolences to the widow.

Then it was my turn. I took the widow's hand and said, "Mrs. Zelnik, I'm Harriet Horowitz. I happened to arrive at the scene of your husband's mur—uh, tragic death. Please accept my deepest sympathies."

"Thank you, sweetheart," she said. She gestured to a young man on her left. "This is my younger son, Aaron."

Then she looked me up and down. "Are you married?" she asked.

Oh, my God. Was she actually trying to fix up her son at her husband's mourning ritual?

"Yes, I am," I replied quickly, attempting what I hoped was an apologetic smile. "I'm so sorry for your loss," I told Aaron, and moved away in haste. I didn't move too far, though, angling to catch some more snatches of conversation. Hopefully relevant ones this time.

I got lucky. The next caller that came along was apparently a close friend of the widow. After she expressed her sympathies, Mrs. Zelnik said, "Oh, come on, Esther. How long have we been friends? Let's get real. You know I'm only doing this for the boys. I wouldn't give that old *shtoonk* the time of day. You know he was *shtupping* half the women in the congregation, and the other half the time he was *farshikkert.*"

Thanks to my long succession of Jewish stepfathers, I'd picked up enough Yiddish to gather that the good rabbi was a skunk, a player and a drunk.

She continued, "I was about to get a *get*—" I knew that was a Jewish divorce "—but the *putz* saved me the trouble."

"Mama, don't talk that way," Aaron interrupted. "Someone might think you killed Papa yourself."

"How dare you speak to your bereaved mother like that," Esther butted in, making a move to smack Aaron. He cowered, covering his face with his hands.

Gee, I wonder why this mama's boy wasn't married yet.

"Oh, please," Mrs. Zelnik said. "Death is too good for him. I planned to take him to the cleaners in the civil divorce. He would have been miserable for the rest of his life for all the suffering he's put me through."

"Besides," Esther said to Aaron, "your mother was playing bridge with me and two other friends all Friday morning. She couldn't have killed your father, even if she'd wanted to. Which, of course, she didn't," she added hastily after the widow gave her a look.

Okay, I'd heard what I'd come for. I headed for the door.

As I rode homeward, my hog humming thanks to the upkeep I'd done, I thought about the widow's alibi. So she had three witnesses to state that she was elsewhere at the time of the murder. But she could have hired a hit man, or woman. But didn't those people usually shoot their target? Strangling someone with his prayer shawl seemed awfully personal. Or spur of the moment.

Just as I pulled the hog up to the airboat, my phone rang.

"Harriet!" It was Lupe. "Have you heard?"

"I've heard plenty, but probably not whatever you have to tell me."

"Oh, it's dreadful."

I got a bad feeling in the pit of my stomach. Unlike my mother, Lupe was no drama queen. If she said something was dreadful, it was.

"Yes?" I asked, almost wincing.

"Father Murphy from Our Lady of the Fairways has been found dead. Drowned in the baptismal font in his own church!"

CHAPTER 18

Now I was absolutely certain that there was a connection among the killings. And damn it, I'd just spent the afternoon pursuing a false lead. I should have trusted my instincts, instead of listening to Mom. Maybe if I had, I could have prevented this latest murder.

I sighed. "Who are the cops pinning it on this time?"

"The church maintenance man. He's Haitian. They found a chicken foot next to the body, so they think he killed the Father as some kind of voodoo sacrifice."

"Say what?"

"Well, you know that animal sacrifices are common voodoo and Santeria practices." As a

cultural anthropologist, Lupe knew all about
these things.

But I knew a few things, too. I knew that chick-
en feet and other animal parts were occasionally
found around town. Especially on the steps of the
courthouse when someone wanted favors from the
deities to influence a case. I also knew about the use
of such dubious devices as Evil-Off Spray and Love
Me Oil. As a ScamBuster, I was well aware that
these were usually cons perpetuated upon desperate, vulnerable believers.

"Yeah, I know about it," I said.

Lupe must have caught the skepticism in my voice.

"You may not believe in it, Harriet, but don't
deny the power of faith. Anyway, human sacrifice
is certainly not part of the picture. Zombification
and casting the evil eye are the preferred methods
of dealing with one's enemies. And only a small
minority of believers practice those dark arts. Plus,
these beliefs are syncretic poly—"

"Sin-cratic-poli? What the hell is that? Shorthand for a sinful theocratic politician? Isn't that redundant?"

"No, Harriet," Lupe said patiently. "*Syncretic polytheistic* religions. Meaning they're a blend, in this case a mix of African Yoruba religions and Catholicism, and they have many gods, which are simply the counterparts of the many saints in Catholicism. So it hardly seems that a Catholic priest would be the target of a killing by these believers."

"So this is obviously another setup," I said.

"Clearly," she replied.

"Thanks for filling me in. I'll get on it."

I turned around and headed straight back to my office. There, I took out my printouts of the committee membership lists that the reverend and the rabbi had both been on. I quickly scanned the lists. Father Murphy was on only one of them, the city council's Ethics Advisory Committee.

This was the only link I could find among the victims. It had to be the key to the crimes.

I went online to look further into the Ethics Committee's activities. I reviewed all the city council minutes for the past year. I nearly passed out from tedium reading about zoning regulations, building permits, contractors' bids, and on and on. However, when I was done, one thing was clear—the Ethics Committee was one influential group.

Over the past year, the committee had made recommendations on about a half-dozen issues. Things like whether to allow a dog racetrack in town, whether to block porn sites from the Internet at the public library and so forth. And in each case, the council ultimately voted in accordance with the committee's recommendation. So if someone wanted to, say, influence the city council on some controversial issue, a good way to do it would be to get to the Ethics Committee.

The killings had to be related, somehow, to one of the three issues that were currently before the committee. I'd already followed the same-sex marriage lead. I'd put the fur fight on the back burner. I decided to keep it there for now. So my next step was obvious. I needed to find out about the internal life of EternaLife.

CHAPTER 19

The next morning I rode to the office and called Preserve-A-Pet, the animal subsidiary of EternaLife.

A dignified male voice answered. "Thank you for calling Preserve-A-Pet, Boca Raton's comprehensive and compassionate pet loss service. How may we help you?"

"It's...it's Buffy, my Siamese," I sniffed. "The vet tells me that..." I sobbed "...that she doesn't have much longer." Now I broke down in tears.

"I understand, my dear," the man said. "It can be unbearable to face the loss of a beloved pet who is like a member of the family. This is a very painful time for you."

"Yes, yes, it is. She's my whole life. We've been together eighteen years. I just can't face the thought of life without her. I heard about your services from a friend, so I'd like to come by and tour your facility to see if it's a suitable place for Buffy to sleep until she can be brought back to life." I sobbed again.

"By all means, my dear. What did you say your name was?"

"Harr…uh, Hailey. Hailey Holloway."

"Ms. Holloway, feel free to come by any time. Of course, the sooner the better. If Barfy—"

"Buffy," I snapped.

"Yes, of course. If Buffy is apt to pass at any moment, it's important to be prepared. She will need to undergo the procedure as soon as possible afterward, so that she may be preserved before, well, decomposition sets in, if you'll pardon my indelicacy."

"Yes, I understand. When she wakes up I want her to be just as she was when she went to sleep. I'd like to come by this morning."

"That will be fine, Ms. Holloway. My name is Robert Barnes, and I will personally guide you through our facility and explain our services."

"Thank you," I sobbed. "I'll see you soon."

I figured preserving your pet wasn't cheap, so I had to dress like someone who could afford it. I packed the old Dolce & Gabbana and its accoutrements into my saddlebags, then rode over to the company.

It was housed in a huge, marble two-story building with neoclassical columns. I cruised past it to a McDonald's, where I went into the restroom and changed. I put on the makeup, smudging the mascara on my lower lids and putting blush on the tip of my nose to make it look as if I'd been crying. The employees all had that fast-food workers' vacant look of boredom coupled with an attitude, and none of them seemed to notice that who had gone into the restroom wasn't the same as who came out.

Outside, I stashed my riding clothes into my saddlebags and then walked over to the pet mausoleum. I pulled open one of the large double doors and stepped into a lushly appointed foyer. The carpeting was a soft blue; the ceiling was painted with blue sky and clouds, and an enormous fresh flower arrangement stood on a round table in the center of the room.

There was no receptionist, but I did see a security camera in one corner of the ceiling so I figured they knew I was there and someone would come out shortly. I sat down on a cushy armchair and waited. Ten minutes later, just as I was about to lose my patience, a short, red-haired, thirtyish man in a black pinstripe suit emerged from the nether regions.

"Hello, how may I help you?" he asked.

"I'm Hailey Holloway. I called earlier."

"Oh, yes, of course, Ms. Holloway. I'm Robert Barnes. Can I offer you something to drink? Espresso? Cappuccino? We have a Sunbucks concession on-site. Of course, this will be on the house."

Sunbucks inside a pet freezing operation? Was no place safe from that coffee empire's insidious plot to take over America?

"Uh, yes, that would be lovely," I said and followed him through a back door. Sure enough, there it was, a full-fledged Sunbucks.

Oh, shit, what was I going to order? I hadn't set foot in one of these bourgeois coffee bars since my Babe days. I wracked my brain to remember the proper insider lingo. Finally, it came to me.

"I'll have a venti double skinny decaf caramel macchiato," I told the Barbie-like barista.

"Certainly. Your name?" she asked, even though no one else was around to confuse her with multiple orders.

"Harr...uh, Hailey."

"Oh, like the comet? That is so cosmic."

She wrote the name on a paper cup, then created the drink and placed it on the other end of the counter, obliging me to walk over, as if there were a line of people waiting behind me.

"Shall we sit down?" Barnes asked.

I nodded and sat.

"Now tell me about...uh...uh..." he stuttered.

"Buffy."

"Yes, of course, Buffy. We've found that talking through one's anticipatory grief is often very therapeutic."

"Oh. Okay, I guess. Buffy was a high-school graduation gift. She's seen me through college, all three marriages, and, of course, she's traveled with me to Paris, London, all over the world, really. She was there for me when all three of my dear husbands passed."

Barnes gulped.

"Yes, poor Dick, Peter and Willy, bless their souls. They're resting in a nice set of matching Wedgwood urns on the mantelpiece of my faux fireplace. But I don't want to go that route with Buffy. I can't stand the thought of her being gone forever."

"Well, you are certainly in the right place, my dear. Allow me to explain our services. Essentially, we will place your beloved companion into a state of suspended animation using the latest cutting-edge technology. This means she will be preserved in pristine condition. Then your faithful friend will be laid in one of our lovely glass enclosures, where you can also place anything you'd like, such as her favorite toys or whatnot. There she will rest in peace. We are open seven days a week from

7:00 a.m. to 10:00 p.m., so you may visit your beloved whenever and as often as you would like. And someday soon, hopefully, the scientific technology will become available to restore her to life."

"So it's kind of like the Sleeping Beauty?"

"Yes, that's it, exactly!"

Like I'd said before, fairy-tale dreams live on in Boca.

"You must understand, however, that we cannot guarantee that such technology will in fact become a reality. It's not as simple as a kiss from a prince to bring your darling out of her sleep. However, the scientific research to date is certainly promising. Nonetheless, our contract does contain a no-guarantee clause."

"Yes, I understand."

"Also, please be aware that we offer a full spectrum of therapeutic services for the bereaved, including counseling, pastoral care, massage therapy, Native American healing circles and much more."

I nodded, not trusting myself to speak.

"Now, Ms. Holloway, as I'm sure you can appreciate, our services are not inexpensive."

"Yes, of course. Money is no object when it comes to my baby. And Dick, Peter and Willy all left me very comfortable."

"Very well, let me explain our price structure. The suspended-animation procedure is ten to twenty thousand dollars, depending on the size of your pet. Since yours is a feline, I imagine it would be at the lower end of that range. Then there's a monthly maintenance fee between five hundred and one thousand dollars, again depending on size. Obviously, larger animals require larger enclosures. And we must keep an extremely low constant temperature within, as you can imagine. Now when it comes to the revivification, the cost of that will have to be determined by market forces at the time the technology becomes available. However, you do have the option to purchase futures on the technology, which would be an excellent investment with a likelihood of very high returns."

Futures on a nonexistent commodity? My Scam-Buster warning system was on high alert. However,

I was here to solve a set of murders, not to bust this bozo. At least not right now.

"That sounds good," I said. Then I sobbed. "I'm sorry, it's just such a dreadful prospect, even though I'm sure your services are wonderful."

"Please, don't apologize. Your feelings are completely natural. Now, here is a sample contract as well as a brochure describing everything I've just explained to you. How about if we take a tour?"

"Yes, I just have a couple questions before we do."

"Certainly."

"Are you the owner of this facility?"

"No, I am the general manager. We are a part of a larger entity, EternaLife."

"Yes, so I've heard. That brings me to my other question. I've heard you're looking to expand into the human arena. Is that so? The reason I ask is, I'm about to be married again, and I'd like to have a plan for my future…well, widowhood."

He gulped again.

"Yes, indeed, you've heard correctly. We're very excited about the proposed expansion. We truly believe this will provide people with a dignified and hopeful alternative to the traditional options. We're currently awaiting approval from the Boca city council. We're quite sure we'll get it, and then we'll be ready to break ground on the new human facility."

"Okay, I'll certainly keep that in mind. I'm ready for that tour now."

We rose and he led me through another door into a large room lined with row upon row of glass display cases. In the center were some benches so that one could sit and contemplate.

The animals and their accompanying enclosures were of varying sizes, ranging from a teacup poodle to a Great Dane. All the dogs and cats did indeed look as if they were peacefully sleeping.

Their owners had clearly spared no expense on their loved ones. Some of the pets delicately rested their heads on Versace pillows; others boasted bejeweled collars; and others had fresh flowers in vases attached to the wall next to each glass case. Almost all the cases held toys, chew bones, catnip and so forth. Damned if this whole thing wasn't like a royal Egyptian tomb. One day, millennia from now, it would be discovered and people would marvel at the bizarre funerary practices of the ancient Boca-ites. A traveling exhibition would be set up—the King Mutt Show—and the bucks would roll in.

"It's lovely," I told Barnes. "Very peaceful."

"Would you like to see the cryonic chamber?"

"Yes."

We proceeded through yet another door into a huge, two-story room dominated by a stainless-steel vat that must have been ten feet tall and eight feet in diameter. A ladder went up the side and a small metal walkway encircled the top.

"Care to go up?" Barnes asked.

"Yes, all right."

"You might want to take those heels off." He nodded toward my feet.

"Yes, you're right." I kicked off the shoes and went up the ladder, with Barnes behind me. I had a feeling he was getting a good view up my skirt.

At the top I stepped onto the walkway, which had railings on both sides. I was now atop the vat, which was covered with a large lid. I moved over so Barnes could join me.

"This is filled with liquid nitrogen," he explained. "It has a temperature of minus 385 degrees Fahrenheit and must be kept under very high pressure to remain in the liquid state."

He pushed a button and the lid slid open. Immediately, gaseous vapors rose up.

"Now, allow me to demonstrate how this works."

He pulled a banana out of his pocket.

"Please feel this," he said.

It had come out of his pants, it was six inches long and slightly curved upward. I did not care for this symbolism at all. However, I did as he asked and touched it. It was ripe and soft.

"Now observe."

Barnes pulled a long piece of string out of his pocket and tied the banana to one end. Then he plunged it down into the vat and pulled it back out immediately.

It was covered with frost, and white vapors evaporated from its surface.

"Let's wait a couple minutes, then touch it again."

I waited and touched. It was cold and solid as a rock.

"That's it," Barnes said. "The basic process of cryonics. As you can see, a couple seconds is all it takes. Of course, some preparation of the body is necessary before the immersion. But we needn't go into those details now."

"Right."

Just then his cell phone rang. "Excuse me," he said and answered it.

After listening for several seconds, he said, "Yes, I'll be right there."

Then to me he said, "I'm so sorry. We've had an arrival. My assistant has just finished prepping it. Would you mind terribly waiting here for just a couple minutes? I'll just get the arrival and bring it right back up here. Then you can see the process in reality."

"Uh, okay," I said, not at all sure I wanted to see some poor creature dipped in there.

"Thank you so much. And please, don't walk

around until I get back. We wouldn't want any accidents."

He sprang down the ladder.

Okay. Sure. I gazed at the vapors rising from the still-open vat. Then, naturally, rebel that I am, I started strolling along the walkway, holding onto both railings.

Suddenly, about halfway around, my feet slipped from under me and beneath the inside railing. The sudden movement caused me to lose my grip on the outer railing. Holy crap! I was barely hanging on to the inner railing with one arm. My body was dangling right over the open vat.

I was about to take a very, very cold plunge.

CHAPTER 20

Thank God, or actually, thank Lior, that my Krav Maga training had given me a buff set of biceps and abs. I grasped the railing with my other arm and did a chin-up. Then I did a lower ab crunch that brought my knees up to the metal walkway. From there I bent to one side and slid my feet, then the rest of me, onto the walkway.

I lay there on my back, my heart pounding. I was sure this was no accident, as Barnes had fore-warned. I touched the walkway next to me. It was slick with some kind of oil. It looked as if Barnes was out to get me. I got up and carefully walked to the ladder, then quickly climbed down.

I looked around the large room and saw a door with a sign saying Emergency Exit: Alarm Will Sound.

Well, my attempted murder certainly qualified as an emergency as far as I was concerned. To hell with the alarm.

I grabbed my high heels off the floor, ran to the door and pushed it open. Sure enough, an alarm sounded. Ignoring it, I got my bearings, then ran through a back alley to the McDonald's where my hog was parked. I grabbed my street clothes out of the saddlebags and ran into the restroom.

If Barnes was out to get me, he probably wouldn't go into a women's room to do it. But what if it wasn't Barnes, but someone else? Like a woman. Could Barbie Barista actually be a covert killer? I decided the restroom really was no refuge.

I ditched the designer duds, pulled on my black uniform and rushed out. I got on my hog, stuffed the suit in the saddlebags and got the hell out of there.

I rode back to the office, my mind, as usual, gaining clarity as I rode. Whoever was out to get me probably wouldn't want to do it in a public place. Both the attacks on me, first in Mort's

Mortuary and now, had been in places where I could easily be disposed of.

It struck me that the methods of disposal were pretty damn ironic. One by burning, the other by freezing.

And the killings of the three clergy seemed tailor-made: an organ pipe for the reverend, a prayer shawl for the rabbi and a baptismal font for the priest. Whoever was behind this was one sick psycho with a sense of humor as twisted as a tornado.

Well, all I had to do was avoid going into any unfamiliar places. Yeah, right. That was gonna happen.

By the time I got back to the office, my fear had turned to fury. I would get this son of a bitch. I'd put up with plenty of threats and violence in my marriage. Never again would I back off from a bully.

I needed to find out more about EternaLife. Such as who owned it. I'd tried obliquely to get the information out of Barnes, but hadn't wanted to push him for fear of making him suspicious of my motives. But obviously, my cover had already been blown. The question was how? And by whom?

Well, if I couldn't squeeze the information out of a person, I just might squeeze it out of the computer. I sat down and logged on to the Internet.

I began with the company's Web site, www.EternaLife.net. I clicked on Who We Are and found the names of a CEO and officers. I recognized some of the names as those who had testified on behalf of the company before the city council, as recorded in the minutes I'd read.

But this didn't tell me who owned the company, just who ran it. Scrolling down farther, I found a statement indicating that EternaLife was a wholly-owned subsidiary of Harbourside Holdings Group. Okay, who the hell was that? Why was nothing ever simple and straightforward? I guess if it was, I'd be out of a job.

I clicked on the link to Harbourside. Again clicking on Who We Are, I found it was a small group of investors who held majority shares in a number of companies throughout South Florida. EternaLife was one of those holdings. Harbourside currently held all the shares because an initial public offering had not been made yet.

Looking through the list of partners, which included six men and two women, I didn't see any names I recognized. Well, hell. More digging was required.

I logged on to a subscription database that provides personal information on everyone in the country: date of birth, current and past addresses, criminal records, property ownership, marriages and divorces and so on. Pretty scary when you think about it, but a great boon to P.I.s.

I printed out the data on all the partners, then sat back, propped my feet on the desk and went through the laborious task of reading it all. Nothing popped up that seemed to have any remote connections to the Ethics Committee or the killings, until I got to the record of one Eileen Stanfield of Bal Harbour, Florida. According to the information, Eileen had married Dennis Pearlman, the vitamin magnate, in Las Vegas about six months ago.

I sat up straight. Finally, something was starting

to come together. And it was big. Since Pearlman
was married to this woman, an investor in Eterna-
Life, he obviously had a financial interest in the
company. Yet he was on the very committee that
was to make a recommendation on EternaLife to
the city council. That was an obvious conflict of
interest that should have led Pearlman to recuse
himself. But he hadn't. Furthermore, he'd recently
made a large charitable contribution to the church
of the Reverend Botay, another committee member. How coincidental was that?

I knew I was finally getting close to the truth. I
had some hunches. I accessed the archives of the
local newspaper to check them out.

First I searched for any mention of Pearlman's
marriage. There was none. Big-time Boca-ite and
publicity hound that he was, this was certainly
unusual. He clearly wanted to leave this liaison off
the public radar.

Next I searched for articles about any other
recent donations he may have made, besides the
one to the Church of the Gender-Free God. As I

expected, these were plentiful and prominent. Among them, three biggies stood out, each for a quarter million dollars. One was to the Temple Beth Boca, for a tutoring program teaming adolescent congregation members with disadvantaged youth from the community. Another was to Our Lady of the Fairways, for a food bank for the homeless. And the third was to the Church of the Serpentine Redeemer, for a seminar series on strengthening marriages.

I could imagine what that last one was all about. I could just see Pastor Hollings preaching, "Wives, submit to your husbands, as they submit to the church." Yep, shut up the women. A great way to strengthen marriages. Why, it had worked for millennia, until those hairy-legged, bra-burning women's libbers had come along and destroyed traditional values. Divine order needed to be restored.

Okay, my hunches were right. Pearlman had a financial interest in EternaLife that he didn't want known. And his "donations" to the religious institutions of the other Ethics Committee members weren't donations at all. They were bribes to get the members to make favorable recommendations for EternaLife.

But since Pearlman had bribed them, why would he then kill them? The killer had to be someone else. I didn't know who yet, but I knew I was hot on the trail.

CHAPTER 21

It was time to go to dinner at Mom's. When I arrived, I saw that Chuck's hog was already there. The would-be newlyweds were back from their would-be wedding trip to San Francisco.

I went in and greeted them with welcome-back hugs. The getaway had apparently done them good. They certainly looked better than the last time I'd seen them.

I said hi to Mom and Leonard. As usual, the two of them and Enrique looked chic in their chichi attire, while Chuck and I looked like outlaws in our riding gear. Just your typical family gathering.

We proceeded outside to the Florida room. For those of you unfortunate non-Floridians, that's a huge screened area, including a screened ceiling, enclosing a pool and patio.

Leonard was grilling chicken in the built-in barbecue pit. Mom excused herself to go to the kitchen to get a salad, sweet potatoes and corn on the cob. Chuck, Enrique and I sat down at the beautifully set table. Enrique immediately took advantage of Mom's absence to grill *me*.

"So what's the status of the investigation?" he asked.

I glanced meaningfully toward the kitchen.

"I'm getting very close to identifying the real killer," I confided. "But I can't tell you any more right now. Trust me, you don't want to see my mom upset again. I'll talk to you later."

"Gotcha," Chuck said, just as Mom returned.

When she sat down, Enrique produced a bottle of wine.

"This is our own special creation," he announced proudly. "We visited a winery in the Napa Valley where they let you make your own blend and put your own label on it. So allow me to present the Boca Bad Boys Estate Bottled Select Reserve. A late harvest blend of one-half each of pinot grigio and pinot noir, both aged in French oak barrels, producing a medium body with a delicate bouquet of vanilla and butter, a hint of fruity and spicy aroma, and an extended finish."

He ceremoniously uncorked the bottle and poured us each a glass.

"*Salute*," he said, raising his glass.

I stared at him. I wasn't about to swallow this swill.

"Are you nuts?" I asked. "You're in the Napa Valley, one of the world's greatest wine regions with expertise going back 150 years. You've got people there that have been making wine for generations. And you think you can do better with some capricious concoction of your own? And who ever heard of mixing a red and a white, anyway?"

"Girlfriend, if I didn't know better, I'd say you have a case of pinot envy," Enrique said and calmly took a sip.

The others followed. I waited a minute. None of

them keeled over, so I raised the glass to my lips and tasted a drop. Then I took a sip and finally a swallow.

"Not bad," I grumbled, avoiding eye contact.

"Well, boys, tell us all about your trip," Mom said.

"Okay," Chuck said. "We started in Haight-Ashbury. I showed Ricky all the hot spots where I hung in the late sixties. I gotta tell y'all, though, the times they are achangin'. What used to be the bead shop is now an Abernathy & Finch clothes store, and the head shop is a Sunbucks coffee shop."

"You're shitting me," I said.

Mom caught my sarcastic tone. "Harriet, what's the matter with you?" she demanded. "Why are you being so antagonistic to the boys?"

"Sorry," I said. "I guess I'm a little on edge today." There'd only been an attempt on my life, that's all. Not that I was going to bring that up and send Mom into drama-queen mode.

"It's no problem, Miz Stella," Chuck said. "We know Harriet is a crusty curmudgeon. We wouldn't have her any other way."

I opened my mouth to make a comeback but thought better of it.

"Anyway," Enrique picked up the story, "then we spent a couple days in the Castro District."

"Excuse me?" I asked, dumbfounded. "You mean to tell me Fidel Castro has an overseas base right here in the U.S.? Do the Miami Cubans know about this?"

Chuck and Enrique looked at each other.

"No, darling," Mom said. "The Castro District is the historic center of gay life in San Francisco. The gay community has done a beautiful job of restoring the old homes to their original Victorian splendor." She smiled proudly.

How did *she* know this stuff? I'd made a fool of myself again with my ex-Boca Babe ignorance. My lack of what seemed to be common knowledge was really starting to bug me. Maybe I needed to get a TV after all. No, scratch that. I'd left behind all those trappings of the Boca Babe life, including the big-screen TV in the media room. They didn't call it the boob tube for nothing. In fact, they might as well call Boca Babes Boob Babes. For more reasons than one. If I wanted to continue my recovery from Babeness and Boobness, I'd better hit the public library instead.

"So as I was saying," Enrique continued, "we went to the Castro. It was awesome to stand on the spot that was one of the major starting points of the gay rights movement back in the day. We've come a long way. But obviously the struggle is far from over."

We sat in silence for a moment, acknowledging the sober truth of that statement.

Then I said, "So you two had a gay old time."

They all groaned.

Leonard came to the table with the platter of chicken. As soon as he sat down and the food was passed around, he launched into his Cold War lore.

"Did I ever tell you all about the time I was involved in Star Wars?" he asked.

"Cool," I said. "Did you get to meet Harrison Ford and Carrie Fisher?"

He blinked. "No, dear, I'm referring to Ronald

Reagan's Strategic Defense Initiative. Back in the early eighties? It was popularly called Star Wars."

Oops, I did it again.

"Oh, yeah, sure, I've heard of that," I said. None of them said a word.

"Well, this program was about developing technology to intercept intercontinental ballistic missiles in space. So, you know, if the Russkies launched a missile at us we'd destroy it before it hit ground."

"Okay," I said.

"The thing is, that technology never actually got *off* the ground. But we fed fake data to the Russkies to make them think the technology was much more advanced than it really was."

"How'd you feed them the fake data?" Enrique asked, sitting on the edge of his seat. As a security specialist, he was the perfect audience for Leonard.

"We passed it to known KGB operatives who we knew would take it back to Moscow. So then the Kremlin was all up in arms, so to speak. In the meantime, what we were really doing was building up our nuclear warheads. So here we've got them thinking we're putting our resources into defense, when it's really offense. Um, preemptive offense, you understand. So they start spending all their budget on getting around our supposed defensive systems. Eventually, that was part of what led to the collapse of their economy."

"Brilliant," Enrique said. Leonard beamed at the praise.

"It's an established strategy, really," he said, trying for modesty. "Straight out of Spying 101. It's called disinformation. You set the enemy on the wrong track to divert them from the truth. Works every time."

"Oh, Leonard, what a clever man you are," Mom gushed. Jeez, this guy really had it made in the admiration department.

Chuck and I silently chowed our chicken.

"And then there was the time I went to Odessa when the entire politburo was there for the winter holiday," Leonard went on. And on.

At last the evening came to a close. We all helped with the dishes, then Chuck, Enrique and

I said our goodbyes to Mom and Leonard and went out to our hogs.

We stood out there in the dark for a while as I quickly filled them in on the investigation. They were not happy, to say the least, about the attempts on my life.

"What kind of whack-job would try to burn you and then freeze you?" Enrique asked.

"I don't know yet. But like I said, I'm getting real close."

"Well, darlin', when you find this weird-ass, we'll take care of him. Or her," Chuck said.

Now, I could understand that sentiment, possessing a justice-obsessed inner vigilante myself. But in all good conscience I couldn't encourage it in others.

"Not a good idea, Chuckles," I said. "The law will take care of the perp."

"Yeah, right," Chuck replied. I guess neither of us was fooled.

"Look guys, it's been real good to see you, but it's been a long day," I said, stifling a yawn. "I'm going to go home and crash, then get back on it tomorrow. As soon as I know more, you'll know."

They reluctantly departed. I put on my helmet and leathers, climbed onto my bike, fired it up and took off toward home.

As I rode through the city streets, glistening under the streetlights from a brief rain, a gloom settled over me. Not only had three victims been brutally murdered, but I now had three suspects to spring, not just the one I'd been hired for. Honey du Mellon/Trey was out on bail, but still facing trial. Since I hadn't heard from Lior, I figured he was still locked up, as was the Haitian maintenance man from Our Lady of the Fairways. Maybe the contessa could get S. Lee Dailey to represent them, but they could still be facing months in jail awaiting trial. I was their only hope. The responsibility weighed heavily on me.

But as I got out of the city and the suburbs and onto the open road, a bikers' saying came to mind: "Wind in my face and my troubles behind, the more I throttle my bike, the more I unwind." I shifted into high gear, opened up the throttle and started to fly. I entered that altered state of consciousness—lost in the moment, hearing the song of the wheels on the road, listening to the pipes talk to me. And when my mind emptied its anxieties, it made room for the truth to enter.

In a flash I knew who the killer was. And more importantly, I knew who the next victim was. And even though I loathed everything the target stood for, I loved justice more. I'd never save his soul. But I had to save his life.

CHAPTER 22

I pulled off the road, pulled out my phone and called the Church of the Serpentine Redeemer. The answering machine came on. I hung up. I turned the bike around and hauled ass over there.

The building was dark. I ran to the door. It was unlocked. Inside, the cavernous meeting hall was unlit. I rushed to Hollings's office. The lights were on and I heard shouts within.

I burst through the door. Hollings and Howard Levine were engaged in a full-on battle. They were both locked in a choke hold, each trying to get the upper hand and throw the other off balance. Along the back wall, the serpents watched from their glass cages.

I pulled my Magnum out of my boot, aimed it at

them, and said, "The BITCH is in the house. You know what BITCH stands for, don't you? Boys, I'm Taking Charge Here. You two get back from each other right now, nice and easy, or you both go down. And trust me, this ain't no girlie gun. You don't want to be on the receiving end of a .44."

"He lets go first," Howard choked out.

"No, he goes first," Hollings replied.

Unbelievable. We were back in kindergarten.

"Boys, I'm going to count to three, and then you both let go together. Are we ready? One…two… three."

They both shoved each other. Hollings caught his balance, but Howard stumbled backward. Right into Monty's aquarium.

The glass shattered as Howard fell on top, and Monty slithered out. The snake went right for Howard's feet, coiling itself around his legs and moving higher. Howard screamed. I aimed and cocked my gun at the beast.

"No!" Hollings yelled. "Don't shoot Monty! I'll

take care of this." He grabbed Monty's head and began talking to him soothingly.

"It's okay, munchkin. You don't need to suffocate this evildoer. He will face his judgment day before our Lord. So let go, sweetie. Daddy's got a nice dinner waiting for you. A couple of big ol' rats. How does that sound?"

Incredibly, Monty began to loosen his grip on Howard's legs.

I kept my gun aimed at all three creatures—Monty, Howard and Hollings.

"Hold it!" I said. I suddenly saw this as a prime opportunity to unravel the murders before Monty unraveled himself. "I want some answers," I said.

Hollings looked from me to Monty to Howard. "Yeah, me, too," he said. "If you don't give it up," he told Howard, "I'll let Monty carry out the Lord's will for you, you heathen."

Amazing. Hollings, the Lord and I were on the same side.

Howard's eyes widened and he swallowed hard.

"Okay," he rasped. "Just keep that viper from squeezing me!"

"Start at the beginning, Howard," I said. "This is all about EternaLife, isn't it? You knew if they set up shop in town, it would seriously cut into your mortuary business, since most Boca residents crave immortality, and have the bucks to buy it. So you had to stop them."

"Of course. And frankly, Harriet, you should be grateful to me for preserving Mort's legacy. You know Mort loved you as if you were his own daughter."

The man was mad. But I decided to play along to keep him talking.

"Yes, Howard, I am grateful. Mort was a good father and a good man, and I'm touched by your loyalty to his memory. Go on."

"Thank you. As I suppose you know, EternaLife was seeking approval from the city council to do business in Boca. The council required a recommendation from its Ethics Advisory Committee before voting on the proposal. So I looked up the Ethics Committee's membership and track record on the Web. I saw that it was a very influential committee. I figured if I could influence the Ethics Committee, they would then sway the council to reject EternaLife. I went to the Reverend Botay first and pitched my proposal—$50,000 in exchange for her recommendation against EternaLife."

Aah. The time-honored tradition of bribery.

"But she declined your offer," I said.

"Not only that, she actually called me crass for offering the money to her personally. Said that personal wealth meant nothing to her. That her life was dedicated to good works. Give me a break."

Howard had made a strategic mistake. If he had offered the money to the church instead of to the reverend personally, that would have made it much more justifiable, in her view, for her to accept the bribe.

"But," Howard continued, "then she added that she'd already received a $250,000 donation to her church, and that out of gratitude to the donor she was going to recommend in favor of EternaLife."

"And you didn't have the finances to make a counteroffer?" I asked.

"No!" Howard yelled, startling Monty, who began to coil tighter around Howard's legs.

"Get him off me!" Howard screamed.

Hollings smiled. "As soon as we have the whole story." He stroked Monty's head and the creature relaxed.

I was still holding up my gun. That sucker is not light. My arm was starting to hurt. I wanted the story wrapped and Monty unwrapped.

"That must have made you really mad," I said to Howard.

"Hell, yes! I left her office. But on the way out, I saw the room next door with the clothes draped over the chairs. So right then I got an idea. I could change, kill the greedy bitch, then change back into my own clothes and dump the bloody ones nearby. I'd be in the clear."

Yeah. And an innocent man would be framed. Real nice.

"So you just grabbed the nearest set of clothes?" Hollings asked.

Howard looked offended. "Of course not. Proper fit is important, my man. I found the clothing that fit best."

Of course. Howard was a natty dresser. And the clothes that fit him best were Trey's. The two of them were about the same size. The other Holy Rollers were taller, shorter, heavier, thinner.

"So you got dressed to kill," I said. "We know the rest."

"What about the rabbi and the priest?" Hollings asked.

"I read the paper, so I knew the donation to the bitch's church came from Dennis Pearlman. He's a filthy rich Boca resident, if you don't know."

"Aren't they all?" Hollings asked.

Howard ignored him. "Then, of course, I realized that Pearlman was behind EternaLife," he continued. "Later I saw on the news that Pearlman had donated the same amounts to the Temple Beth Boca and Our Lady of the Fairways. Of course, I recognized those donations as bribes. So I killed the others, too. I just hid in the temple and the church and waited for them to arrive. Just like I hid here, waiting for you, my dear pastor. I knew you would come sooner or later, whether tonight or in the morning. But Harriet here screwed up my plans."

Obviously, the man had gone nuts. Having seemingly gotten away with the first murder, he felt omnipotent and kept on killing.

I'd heard enough. And my arm was real tired.

"Call the cops, for God's sake," I told Hollings.

He may have had God and Monty, but I had the gun. He did as I said. The cops came, took statements from all of us, then hauled Howard off in cuffs. Hollings and I were left looking at each other.

"Young lady, you saved my life," he said. "For that you have my respect."

"The feeling isn't mutual," I assured him, and got the hell out of that snake pit.

CHAPTER 23

Two days later, the entire wedding party and guests reconvened at the Hog Heaven biker bar. Chuck and Enrique, all five Holy Rollers, Mom' and Leonard, the contessa and Coco, Lupe and I all sat at a couple of tables that had been pushed together. Also there were Lior and Pierre Laboisse, the Haitian maintenance man, both of whom had been released, their charges dropped, after Howard had confessed to the police. The rest of the place was filled with the remaining guests, including Chuck's biker customers and the gay matchmaker and his clients. And S. Lee Dailey had shown up as well.

Immediately after Howard's arrest, I'd called Cherise Jubilee, then Chuck and Enrique. I briefly filled them in, then told them that I wasn't going to repeat the story over and over to all the interested parties, so a group gathering was called for. Chuck and Enrique had already booked and paid for the Hog Heaven for their reception, so they'd called the owner, who graciously changed the date. And the agenda was changed from a marriage reception to a murder recitation.

The party menu remained unchanged, so everyone, even Mom and the contessa, was guzzling beer and downing buffalo wings, onion rings and fried mozzarella sticks. The jukebox was playing a collection of country songs that someone had evidently deemed appropriate in view of the vocations of the murder victims: "Drop Kick Me Jesus Through the Goalposts of Life"; "I Been Roped and Thrown by Jesus in the Holy Ghost Corral"; and "Thank God and Greyhound She's Gone".

My favorite bartender, Marla, came over with a tray full of beer bottles. As usual, she wore a black leather halter, and her long gray hair hung down her back in a braid. Her face was lined and wrinkled from years of the hard life. But something about her looked different. Some kind of light shined out from her usually dull eyes.

"Hey, Marla, what's up?" I asked. "You're looking…good. Uh, I mean, more relaxed, happier."

"I finally kicked out my ol' man," she said in her gravelly smoker's voice.

"Get out of town!" I said. Her ol' man was a habitually unemployed, verbally abusive, lying drunk. I'd urged—okay, told her—to dump his useless ass, but she'd refused, saying he did have one use—in bed.

"No, honey, I'm serious as a heart attack," she said.

"So what was the last straw?"

"The booze finally poisoned him so much that he got…whaddya call it? Oh, yeah, erectile dysfunction."

"Oh." I wasn't sure I wanted that much information. "So not only was he a pathological liar, he was a pathological lover."

"Yep, you got it. So I told him, 'Hey, you can't get it up, there's no hard feelings. Just zip up, shut up, pack up and clear out.'"

"What'd he say?"

"He goes, 'But, baby, I can get me some Viagra.' So I said, 'Go ahead. I hope it gets stuck in your throat and gives you a stiff neck.'"

"Uh-huh."

"And you know what? I really am happier. Right now all I want is a meaningful overnight relationship."

"Uh, yeah, right," I said. "Well, I'm really happy for you."

"Thanks, hon," she said, and left to serve another table.

Marla's newfound independence reminded me that you can't force anyone to see the light. Marla had found her own truth and a new strength within herself. Whether my unsolicited advice to her had had anything to do with that, I didn't know. Maybe I'd planted the seed, maybe not.

I thought back to Brigitta Larsen O'Malley. She'd actually asked for my advice, then ignored it. But maybe one day, like Marla, and like me, she would find that seed of strength inside herself and cultivate it, until a whole new life broke through the soil of fear and blossomed in the fresh air of freedom.

As the meal wound down, Lior rose and nodded at Marla, who turned off the jukebox. Suddenly the room was silent and all eyes were on Lior. To my horror, he started to make a toast in my honor.

"Friends, let us raise our glasses—um, that is, bottles—to the incomparable Harriet Horowitz. A woman whose brains, courage, heart and devotion to the pursuit of justice are unsurpassed. And I want all of you to know that while she pursues justice, I will pursue her with the same devotion."

How embarrassing was this? I put on a tight smile.

Enrique elbowed Chuck. "What do we say? What's that Jewish thing they say?"

Chuck shrugged.

"I know what it is, I know what it is," Enrique muttered. "Ma…Matzo…Maz…Yeah, I got it! Mazel tov!" he yelled. Everyone cheered.

Then, to my further horror, some of the guests lifted up my chair, with me in it, and passed me around the room above their heads. Some of these people weren't exactly sober. I didn't exactly trust them not to drop me. But I could hardly let my fear show after what Lior had just said about my courage. So I grinned and bore it as they bore me to the front of the room.

Finally they set the chair down. On top of the bar. Somebody handed me a microphone.

Great, just great. Here I was, like the pontiff on his balcony preaching to the masses below. Well, maybe this wasn't so bad. When would I get another chance to pontificate like this?

"Dearly beloved," I began. "I've gathered you here today to explicate the murders of our cherished spiritual leaders, the Reverend LaVerne Botay, Rabbi Lev Zelnik and Father Patrick Murphy."

Okay, so maybe the rabbi wasn't cherished quite by all, but it certainly wasn't my place to reveal his widow's feelings. I proceeded to explain the hows and whys of the killings.

"So this wasn't about the gay marriage ordinance at all?" someone asked when I'd finished.

"Right. This wasn't about marital legislation, it was about market competition. The market being the dead. And that's all, folks."

I got up, hopped off the bar and went back to my table. Marla started the jukebox again and the guests resumed partying.

"That was a very good presentation, Harriet," the contessa said. "But we know that's not all there is. I can understand that you did not want to share all the details with everyone. But now that you're among family and friends, give us the full, un-abridged version."

"Like what?" I asked.

"Like, how did you figure out Howard was the killer?" Cherise Jubilee asked.

I turned to Leonard. "It was you who finally put me on the right track," I told him.

"Really? How?" Leonard asked as Mom patted his knee and gazed at him adoringly.

"Remember the other night at dinner, when you were talking about the technique of disinformation?"

"Yeah, sure."

"Well, I realized Howard was feeding me disinformation. Through Mom. Sorry," I said to her.

"What do you mean?" she asked. "I'm already in such disbelief that my dear friend has turned out to be a killer. I feel so deceived. And you mean there's more to it?"

"I'm afraid so. There were a couple times during my investigation when you suggested possible leads to follow. The first was when you said that the reverend's killer might be someone who had a beef with Trey over a court case. That led me to Lucas Morse and the Loyal Brotherhood of Ass—uh, Aryans. The second time was when you suggested I check out the rabbi's wife as a potential suspect. Both of those turned out to be false leads. They derailed me off the track. After Leonard talked about disinformation, I realized that both of the times you suggested those leads were after you'd spoken with Howard. He got you involved in the iguana protests just to have the opportunity to feed you false information. He was using you as a stooge. I'm sorry, Mom."

She looked crestfallen. Leonard squeezed her hand.

"You're right, Harriet," she said. "Howard did give me those ideas. I'd told him there was some friction between you and me, and he suggested that I might improve my relationship with you if I was helpful to your investigation. I only meant well. I had no idea he was using me."

"It's all right, Mom. He played on your vulnerability. He was a smooth operator. You can't blame yourself for not seeing what was really going on. After all, I didn't see it myself. And maybe I still wouldn't if Leonard hadn't brought up the disinformation thing. I didn't catch on to Howard's lies even from the start, when I ran into him at the city council meeting. He told me he was there regarding the iguana-bridge issue. That was a lie. He wasn't there about the iguanas. He was really there about EternaLife. He wanted to throw me off track. And he did, because I left the meeting before EternaLife came up. I didn't learn about it until much later."

"That's okay, darlin'," Chuck said.

"Yeah, you still rock," Enrique added.

That was nice of them to say. But I still felt guilty. If I'd just stayed at that meeting longer, maybe I would have gotten on the right track sooner and prevented the two subsequent killings. I guess I'd carry that regret with me to my grave—or urn, or suspended state, or whatever.

"There's one more thing, Harriet," Virginia Hamm said. "When you briefed us, you mentioned offhandedly that you'd been endangered a couple times during the investigation. What's up with that?"

"What?" Mom exclaimed. "Why didn't you tell me about this, Harriet?"

"I think the reason is obvious. I didn't want to upset you, just like you are now. Anyway, it's over. I'm safe, so you can chill."

"Well, I never…" Mom started, but Leonard clutched her hand, and she sat back in silence and pouted.

I recounted how I'd been shoved into and then rescued from the casket in Howard's funeral home. Everyone at the table was aghast.

"Naturally, I thought that whoever shoved me in there wanted me dead and they didn't know that that casket wasn't going into the cremation oven. But now I realize that it was Howard who shoved me in there in the first place. He knew that casket wasn't going in. He didn't want to kill me, just scare me. I guess he had some shred of conscience since his partner Mort was my stepfather and Howard has known me since I was in high school. And by 'rescuing' me he also set himself up as a good guy, so I wouldn't suspect him of anything later."

Mom started sniffling. "I just cannot believe that our family friend, whom Mort loved like a brother, could do such things."

"I know, Mom. Being betrayed by someone you trust is a stab right in the heart."

Mom nodded.

"What about the other attack?" Lupe asked.

"That was a similar scenario. Except this time it wasn't Howard. It was Dennis Pearlman. I'd gone to interview him at his vitamin company. So immediately he knew I posed a threat to his bribery scheme. He wanted to keep track of me. He got my image from the security cameras in his building. Then he transmitted it over to Preserve-A-Pet and instructed his minion over there, Barnes, to keep close watch on *their* security cameras to see if I came in. If I did, he was supposed to scare me off some way. So sure enough, I came in and he recognized me, even though I was undercover."

I described my slip off the platform of the liquid nitrogen vat.

"Barnes had put this oily substance on the platform. The thing is, he was supposed to be walking around there with me, and when I slipped he was supposed to rescue me. Then he was supposed to issue a warning for me to back off from EternaLife. So Pearlman, like Howard, just wanted to scare me, not kill me. But the plan went awry when Barnes was unexpectedly called away and I walked around the platform myself. So I nearly *was* killed, but I was able to save myself."

I looked at Lior. "Thanks to your fitness training," I told him.

"That's my girl!" he said.

I glared at him. "Girl? Yours? No. I am a woman, and I'm no one's possession."

Lior rolled his eyes heavenward. "Nothing I say to her is right. Why, Lord, am I tortured like this? Why do I want her like no other woman?"

"Kids, kids, please," Enrique said. "The road to romance can be rocky. Sometimes that makes it all the more exciting."

Chuck grunted. Lior and I both bit our tongues.

Keisha LaReigne broke the silence. "How did you figure out Pearlman was only trying to scare you?" she asked.

"I didn't. The cops had a chat with Barnes and when they mentioned an attempted-murder charge, he squealed on Pearlman. And by the way, I think Pearlman figured out what Howard was up to and had one of his goons push Howard off the bridge to scare *him* off. But that's something we'll never know for sure. With all the people on that bridge that night, there's no way to prove it wasn't just an accident."

"So none of this had anything to do with homophobia, or racism, or anti-Semitism or anything like that," Honey du Mellon summed up.

"That's right," I said. "Obviously, those kinds of bigotry are in no short supply around here. But in the end, there's really only one thing that moves Boca, which we all should have known from the start."

"Money," everyone said simultaneously.

EPILOGUE

It was a couple weeks later. I was sitting in my rocking chair on my porch, sipping my Hennessy and waiting for Lana to come home so I could tell her about my day.

She finally floated into view.

"It's about time," I said. "I've got some big news to tell you."

"Give it up, girl!" she said.

"Today the city council voted on EternaLife and the same-sex marriage ordinance. I attended the meeting."

"And?"

"First of all, the council had appointed a new Ethics Committee. In accordance with that committee's recommendations, EternaLife is out and same-sex marriage is in."

Lana flipped her tail back and forth in delight.

"So Chuck and Enrique can get married now. Legally. And, the Church of the Gender-Free God has a new minister, the high priestess of Lupe's coven. So the wedding is rescheduled for next month."

"Yesss!" If Lana could have pumped a fist in the air, she would have. "Speaking of romance," she went on, "what's the latest on Lior?"

"Lior? Um… We're still stumbling down the perilous path of…passion."

"Well, now that you've proven he's not a killer— not in this case, anyway—you have my permission to keep stumbling."

"Gee, thanks."

We were silent for a while as I reflected on my relationship with Lior. Okay, so we'd become closer. And not just physically. Maybe I did sort of, well, care for him. I'd gone to jail after him. Hell, isn't that how all meaningful relationships start out?

And as for our age gap, I seemed to be thinking about it less and less as I knew him more and more.

The case had affected my other relationships, too. Howard's exploitation of the tensions between Mom and me had brought us a little closer—neither of us wanted to be vulnerable to outside forces like that again. So it seemed that lately, we kind of agreed to disagree on some things, instead of blowing up at each other.

And I'd made a whole new set of friends in the Holy Rollers. I had to face it: my post-Babe life was evolving in ways I'd never expected. When I'd retreated to my Glades hideaway following my abusive marriage, it wasn't loneliness I'd feared. It was relationships. Now I was entangled in them. The fear was still there, but now I was facing it.

"Hey," Lana broke into my thoughts. "I've been wondering, whatever happened to Levine and Pearlman?" she asked.

It took me a second to get back to the moment. "Oh. Howard pleaded insanity. In view of his confession, the D.A. decided to forgo a trial and accept the plea. Howard will be a guest of the state hospital for a long, long time."

"And Pearlman?"

"The only thing that happened to him was he was removed from the Ethics Committee because of his conflict of interest. But his wife and the whole Harbourside group are being investigated by the Securities and Exchange Commission for selling those bogus EternaLife futures.

"As for my slip on the nitrogen vat, he claimed it was an accident. It was his word against Barnes's, so it couldn't go anywhere. And as for the bribes, no one can prove that's what they were. After all, it was Howard who claimed that, and then he claimed insanity. So there's no way to show they're anything but charitable donations. And even if it could be proven they were bribes, Pearlman didn't bribe elected officials, only appointed committee members. That's not a crime. It's the good old American way—lobbying. The worst that could be said is that the Ethics Committee members were unregistered lobbyists. But they're dead, anyway."

"And what about Hollings and the Loyal Brotherhood of Assholes?" Lana asked.

"Still preaching their gospel of hatred, practicing their First Amendment rights. Morse was found guilty of painting that swastika on the Temple Beth Boca. He might do a few months for the swastika incident, but that's it."

"Wow," Lana said.

I sat there and she floated there, both of us contemplating the vicissitudes of justice and injustice, morality and immorality, life and death.

"You know what, Lana?" I finally asked.

"What?"

"There's something I've learned from all this. Hollings was right about one thing."

"Huh?" she asked incredulously.

"He said we're all sinners. And he was right. Even the Reverend Botay, as wonderful as she was, wasn't a saint. She succumbed to Pearlman's proposal. She sold her vote on the Ethics Committee in exchange for his donation to her battered women's program. I guess she figured she was serving the greater good. So where do we draw the line? Are there good sins and bad sins? Justifiable and unjustifiable? Forgivable and unforgivable?"

We sat and floated in silence again.

"I don't know," Lana finally said, echoing my own thoughts. "All we can do is move forward, continuing our crusade for truth and justice, elusive though they may be at times."

"Wait a minute," I said. "*Our* crusade?"

"Yeah. You and me, sister. Together. Forever."

We locked eyes.

"Yeah," I said. "Together. Love ya, sis."

"Right back atcha," she said and floated off into the sunset.

* * * * *

Be sure to return to NEXT in September
for more entertaining women's fiction
about the next passion in a woman's life.
For a sneak preview of Nancy Robards Thompson's
THE BLONDE LEADING THE BLONDE,
coming to NEXT in September,
please turn the page.

Today, as I fly out of LAX, probably for the last time, the souvenirs I'm taking with me are two truths I gleaned doing hair in the Hollywood movie industry: (1) appearance is everything; and (2) reality, that eternal shape-shifter, is the biggest illusion of all.

Reality is ninety-nine-point-nine percent perception. It morphs and changes into whatever form best moves ahead the perceiver.

As I, Avril Carson, thirty-five-year-old widow of Chet, and *former* aspiring-starlet-turned-Hollywood-stylist, wipe my clammy palms on my Dolce & Gabbanas (which I bought gently worn at a consignment shop for a fraction of the retail price—but no one needs to know that) and prepare to speed into the wild blue yonder into the next chapter of my life, witness Hollywood truths one and two play out in real life.

It goes like this: even though I loathe flying, I've convinced myself that I *must* fly across the country because the alternative is to come rolling back home into Sago Beach, Florida, in a Greyhound bus.

No can do. Ride the bus, that is.

But I *hate* to fly. If I were being completely real, I'd keep my feet on the ground and take that bus— body odor be damned—over hurling through the air from one coast to the other.

Chet would've been proud of me for venturing so far out of my comfort zone. I press my leg against my carry-on, which holds the box of his ashes, hoping to absorb some of his courage.

Chet Marcus Carson, extreme sports reporter for WKGM Hollywood. Nothing scared him, which is part of the reason he's dead…nine months now. Parasailing accident.

And now, Chet Marcus Carson is the reason I'm going home. I tried my best to stick it out on my own, but, by the time I lost Chet, the Hurray-For-Hollywood-rose-colored-glasses were gone.

I arrive at my seat and remind myself that today, I'm only supposed to think positive thoughts.

A man pauses in the aisle beside me.

"Excuse me, I think I'm sitting next to you." He removes a black cowboy hat, glances at his boarding pass and gestures to the vacant middle seat. "Row 25? Seat B?"

The guy is tall—maybe six-four. The manly-man variety that takes up lots of space. The type who sprawls and hogs both armrests.

Great.

Later, as the engines roar, and the plane taxies down the runway, I'm gripped by the third Hollywood truth: when bullshit fails, backpedal like hell and disassociate yourself from the lie as fast as you can.

The words, Let me out of this death trap! gurgle up in my throat, but even if I could find my voice, it's too late. The plane lifts off. The g-forces press me into the seat like invisible hands hell-bent on pinning me down.

I hug myself and squeeze my eyes shut. My breath comes in short, quick gasps.

"Oh, God. Oh, God. Oh, God. Oh, God!"

"Are you okay?" the cowboy asks.

"Takeoff's my favorite part of the flight."

Huh?

I open one eye and look at the cowboy. Not only is he taking up both armrests, he's listing in my direction.

He's so much bigger than Chet, who was lean, and fair and Hollywood fabulous. The cowboy is dark and good looking if you like a raven-eyed-five-o'clock-shadow-feral-looking-Tim-McGraw sort of man. I shift away from his manliness.

"There's always so much possibility when a plane takes off." He has one of those piercing, look-you-in-the-eyes kind of gazes. "It's so symbolic. New places. New beginnings. New opportunities. What's your favorite part of the ride?"

My mouth is dry, but I manage to say, "When they open the door to the gate. Now leave me alone so I can go to sleep. My Dramamine is kicking in."

MIRACULOUSLY, I DO MANAGE to sleep most of the nonstop flight. My eyes flutter open to the sound of the flight attendant's announcement asking everyone to secure their tray tables and return their seats to the upright position as we prepare to land in Orlando.

I stretch and rub my stiff neck.

"See, that wasn't so bad, was it?" says the cowboy. "The worst part is over."

Hollywood truths one and two kick in and I want to believe him.

Yeah, now that I'm home the worst is just about over.

I believe that for about fifteen minutes—until we deplane and make our way to baggage claim where my mother and half the population of Sago Beach are standing under a banner that proclaims, "Welcome home, Avril! Sago Beach's very own beauty operator to the stars."

REQUEST YOUR FREE BOOKS!

2 FREE NOVELS PLUS 2 FREE GIFTS!

There's the life you planned. And there's what comes next.

YES! Please send me 2 FREE Harlequin® NEXT™ novels and my 2 FREE mystery gifts. After receiving them, if I don't wish to receive any more books, I can return the shipping statement marked "cancel." If I don't cancel, I will receive 4 brand-new novels every other month and be billed just $3.99 per book in the U.S. or $4.74 per book in Canada, plus 25¢ shipping and handling per book plus applicable taxes, if any.* That's a savings of over 25% off the cover price! I understand that accepting the 2 free books and gifts places me under no obligation to buy anything. I can always return a shipment and cancel at any time. Even if I never buy anything from Harlequin, the two free books and gifts are mine to keep forever.   155 HDN EL33   355 HDN EL4F

Name _____ (PLEASE PRINT) _____

Address _____ Apt. # _____

City _____ State/Prov. _____ Zip/Postal Code _____

Signature (if under 18, a parent or guardian must sign)

Order online at www.TryNEXTNovels.com

Or mail to the **Harlequin Reader Service®:**

IN U.S.A.: P.O. Box 1867, Buffalo, NY 14240-1867
IN CANADA: P.O. Box 609, Fort Erie, Ontario L2A 5X3

Not valid to current Harlequin NEXT subscribers.

Want to try two free books from another line?
Call 1-800-873-8635 or visit www.morefreebooks.com

* Terms and prices subject to change without notice. NY residents add applicable sales tax. Canadian residents will be charged applicable provincial taxes and GST. This offer is limited to one order per household. All orders subject to approval. Credit or debit balances in a customer's account(s) may be offset by any other outstanding balance owed by or to the customer. Please allow 4 to 6 weeks for delivery.

Your Privacy: Harlequin Books is committed to protecting your privacy. Our Privacy Policy is available online at www.eHarlequin.com or upon request from the Harlequin Reader Service. From time to time we make our lists of customers available to reputable firms who may have a product or service of interest to you. If you would prefer we not share your name and address, please check here. ☐

NEXT07R

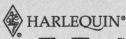
HARLEQUIN®

Next™

GET $1.00 OFF

your purchase of any Harlequin NEXT novel.

Receive $1.00 off
any Harlequin NEXT novel.

Available wherever books are sold, including most bookstores, supermarkets, drugstores and discount stores.

Coupon expires January 31, 2008.
Redeemable at participating retail outlets
in the U.S. only. Limit one coupon per customer.

RETAILER: Harlequin Enterprises Ltd. will pay the face value of this coupon plus 8 cents if submitted by the customer for this specified product only. Any other use constitutes fraud. Coupon is nonassignable. Void if taxed, prohibited or restricted by law. Void if copied. Consumer must pay any government taxes. Mail to Harlequin Enterprises Ltd., P.O. Box 880478, El Paso, TX 88588-0478, U.S.A. Cash value 1/100 cents. Limit one coupon per customer. Valid in the U.S. only.

5 65373 00076 2   (8100) 0 11435

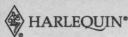

HARLEQUIN®

NeXt™

GET $1.⁰⁰ OFF

your purchase of any
Harlequin NEXT novel.

Receive $1.⁰⁰ off

any Harlequin NEXT novel.

*Available wherever books are sold, including
most bookstores, supermarkets, drugstores
and discount stores.*

Coupon expires January 31, 2008.
Redeemable at participating retail outlets
in Canada only. Limit one coupon per customer.

52608038

HARLEQUIN®

Mediterranean
NIGHTS™

Experience glamour, elegance, mystery and revenge
aboard the high seas....

Coming in September 2007...

BREAKING ALL
THE RULES

by

Marisa Carroll

Aboard the cruise ship *Alexandra's Dream* for
some R & R, sports journalist Lola Sandler is
surprised to spot pro-golfer Eric Lashman.
Years after walking away from the pro circuit
with no explanation to the public, Eric now
finds himself teaching aboard a cruise ship.

Lola smells a career-making exposé...
but their developing relationship may
force her to make a difficult choice.

HARLEQUIN®

COMING NEXT MONTH

#91 DOCTOR IN THE HOUSE • Marie Ferrarella

Having taken several wrong turns in her own life,
Bailey DelMonico is passionate about her new career as a
doctor. And she has resolved not to let other "passions"
interfere. That is until she is paired with the sharp-tongued
Dr. Ivan Munro. Skilled at saving patients' lives, this
arrogant doctor doesn't know how to save himself from the
isolated existence he's created. In reaching out to Ivan,
Bailey is about to discover that there are many ways to save
a life…and it's never too late for love.

#92 BEAUTY SHOP TALES •
Nancy Robards Thompson

Washed-up "beauty operator to the stars" Avril Carson
left L.A. for a fresh start in her Florida hometown—only
to discover an explosive secret between her deceased
husband and her best friend. Suddenly Avril's new life had
scandal, betrayal, even a handsome hunk waiting in the
wings, whom she'd met on the plane ride home. And she'd
thought her days of Hollywood-style drama were over!